Friends for Life

Ellen Emerson White

AN AVON  FLARE BOOK

Blairsville High School Library

FRIENDS FOR LIFE is an original publication of Avon Books. This
work has never before appeared in book form.

AVON BOOKS
A division of
The Hearst Corporation
105 Madison Avenue
New York, New York 10016

Copyright © 1983 by Ellen Emerson White
Published by arrangement with the author
Library of Congress Catalog Card Number: 82-90806
ISBN: 0-380-82578-3
RL: 5.5

All rights reserved, which includes the right to reproduce this book or
portions thereof in any form whatsoever except as provided by the U.S.
Copyright Law. For information address the Walter Pitkin Literary
Agency, 11 Oakwood Drive, Weston, Connecticut 06883.

First Avon Flare Printing: March 1983

AVON FLARE TRADEMARK REG. U.S. PAT. OFF. AND IN OTHER COUNTRIES,
MARCA REGISTRADA, HECHO EN U.S.A.

Printed in the U.S.A.

RA 10 9 8

To my parents, for all their support; my agent, for taking on the manuscript in the first place; my editor, for trying to make something out of it; and most of all, to my grandmother, Dorothy Dorr White, because I love her.

CHAPTER ONE

Susan McAllister climbed up to the second floor of her new duplex apartment, carrying two too many boxes. She felt her way along the hall to her bedroom, the first door on the right. Her cocker spaniel, Murdoch, ran along next to her, panting and wagging his tail.

"Hey, cut it out," she said as he grabbed her jeans leg between his teeth, growling in that way that sounded like laughing. "Murdoch, come on, down!" She tried to shake him loose and balance the boxes at the same time, managing to misjudge the position of her bed and crash into the footboard, losing the top two boxes. She frowned at the mess of books and papers, then let the other two boxes fall. Murdoch barked, pawing her leg, the wagging tail shaking his entire body. "I bet you think that's funny."

She patted him, sitting down on the highly varnished floor to clean up. The real estate agent had told her parents that these were the original hardwood floors from the sixteenth century or whenever it was that people—Pilgrims?—had started building on Beacon Hill. Judging from the way all the floors seemed to tilt, it was probably true.

"Susan?" her mother called from the bottom of the stairs. "Colleen's here."

"I'm in my room," Susan called back. She paused, a pile of books and Murdoch on her lap, listening to the light, familiar steps. She had known Colleen since they were seven, which made it . . . ten years?

It didn't seem like ten years. God, they were getting old. Anyway, in all that time Colleen had always sounded the same on the stairs: quick, confident and as though she had never tripped. All three were true. Listening to the steps, it seemed almost as though she and her family had never moved away, as though she were fourteen again and her father had never been transferred to the branch office in Manhattan. Of course he had been and they had been in New York for the last three years—until he had been promoted and transferred back to Boston. Hearing Colleen now made it seem as though they had never left.

"Hi." Colleen appeared in the doorway, smiling that "is-there-a-camera-in-the-room-or-was-it-my-imagination?" smile, still hanging on to the tan she had acquired in Florida during Christmas vacation. Susan reflected vaguely on the fact that while they were both wearing sweatshirts and jeans, Colleen looked well-dressed. It could be that her sweatshirt fit; it was new, light purple and very stylish. Susan looked down at her own sweatshirt that was grey with a faded crimson "Harvard" lettered across the front and belonged to her father.

"Hi," she answered. "Thought you were coming over around ten."

"Huh?" Colleen squinted at Susan's clock-radio, which said eleven-fifteen. "Guess I got held up." Her eyebrows came together for a second, then she smiled again. "So, what can I do to help?"

"God, I don't even know." Susan scanned the mass of books, papers and clothes, then shuddered. "Was it this bad when we moved away?"

"Worse."

"Hard to believe." She looked at her friend, noticing how thin she was. Usually you just saw the blond hair and tan and didn't look any further, just assuming healthy, All-American beauty. She was thin though, much too thin. Her cheekbones seemed almost sharp and her eyes were strangely bright.

8

"Are you on another one of those stupid diets?"

"No." Colleen checked herself. "Why?"

"You look kind of anorexic."

"I'm just tired."

"You look it." Susan frowned. "What's wrong?"

"Nothing."

"Nothing?"

"Yeah, nothing." Colleen's voice was irritated. "I'm fine."

"You sure?"

"Susan!"

"Okay, sorry." Susan lifted Murdoch off her lap and stood up, putting her hands in her pockets. "You just don't look that great."

"Look," Colleen lifted her hair off her shoulders, holding it up against the back of her head with one arm. "You've been here only since yesterday. I don't feel like going into it."

"So something *is* wrong."

Colleen dropped her arm, letting her hair fall, and sat down on the bed.

"I'm fine," she said. "What can I do to help?"

"God, I don't know." Susan kicked at one of the boxes. "I can't even figure out where to start. You want to help me put the books away?"

"Yeah, sure." Colleen got up and they started carrying piles over to the white bookcase built into the far wall.

They worked quietly for a few minutes, Colleen setting aside the books she wanted to borrow, a stack that was growing almost as big as the stack in the bookcase.

"Do you think I take things too seriously?" she asked suddenly.

"Like what?" Susan glanced up from the row of Hemingway.

"I don't know." Colleen studied a copy of *The Sound and the Fury.* "Everything. Do you think I'm—obsessive?"

9

"Yeah."

"But I'm not."

"Yeah, you are," Susan shrugged. "You always have been."

"But I'm not. I just—" Colleen let out a hard breath. "I don't know. Sometimes I think things are important."

"What are you talking about?"

"I don't know." Colleen sat down, her expression unhappy. "I got yelled at this morning. My parents think I'm obsessive."

"You are."

Colleen scowled, slouching down, her arms across her chest.

"Why do they think so?" Susan sat down on another box. "Just in general?"

"I don't know." Colleen slouched lower. "Just forget it."

"Forget it?" Susan shook her head. "You're really weird, you know that?"

"Why should I tell you?" Colleen's arms tightened against her sweatshirt. "You'll just think I'm crazy too."

"I'm your best friend. I won't think you're crazy."

"Yeah, they're my parents."

"Come on." Susan leaned forward to touch her friend's arm. "Tell me."

Colleen looked at her, then nodded.

"Okay," she said. "Remember the guy at my school I told you about? The one who showed up dead of an overdose?"

"Yeah, what about it?"

"It was murder."

"What?"

"It was murder."

"Are you kidding?"

Colleen shook her head.

"Oh." Susan sat back, leaning against the wall, her arms folding.

10

"See? You don't believe me either." Colleen crossed to the window, gripping the sill with both hands, staring out at the snow-covered sidewalks of Chestnut Street.

"Well," Susan shifted her position, "what makes you so sure?"

"He didn't take drugs."

"How do you know?"

"I know, okay? He just didn't. I mean maybe he smoked pot but nothing that would have killed him." She pushed hard against the sill, staring outside, and Susan could see her arms trembling.

"Well," Susan shifted again, "who did it?"

"I don't know."

"Do you have a motive?"

"I'm not sure."

Susan didn't say anything more and Colleen turned around, her face tight.

"You want to listen?" she asked, "or make fun of me?"

"I didn't make fun of you," Susan said defensively. "It just sounds—I don't know. We stopped playing 'Detective' when we were eleven, remember?"

"Yeah, well, you know how immature I am." Colleen turned back to the window, hands clenching on the sill again. "Let's forget it, okay? I'm sorry I mentioned it. What makes you different from anyone else?"

"Colleen, I'm sorry."

"It doesn't matter."

"It does matter. Come on, tell me."

"It's just . . ." Colleen sighed, letting her arms relax. "I knew him, Susan. It doesn't make sense. The whole drug thing at our school is really quiet and—well, what if he had found out something? What if—I don't know. But people sure don't want to talk about it. The more I find out, the more—"

"I thought you said people weren't talking."

11

"I have my sources," Colleen said shortly. "Let's drop it."

"Sure." Susan picked up a copy of *A Separate Peace* and started flipping through it. "Whatever you say."

"I'm sorry. I didn't mean to take it out on *you.*"

Susan continued turning pages, reading the beginning of the fourth chapter.

"Come on, don't be mad," Colleen said.

"I'm not."

Colleen laughed for the first time since she had arrived. "Yeah, you are," she said. "You feel like hitting me."

"I do not." Susan saw her friend's grin and she had to grin back. "Well, maybe a little." She put *A Separate Peace* on one of the shelves. "What do the police think about all of this?"

"Oh, them." Colleen's smile left. "They think I'm crazy. Everyone thinks I'm crazy." She hesitated. "What do you think?"

"Well." Susan hesitated too. "I don't know."

"You think I'm crazy."

"I'm not sure."

"At least you're always honest." Colleen walked over to Susan's desk, lifting up a pile of books. She let out her breath, putting them back down. "You have no idea how much I've missed you."

"Yeah, I do."

"Yeah?" Colleen looked at *Ethan Frome,* then at Susan. "Can you try to believe me? I really need someone to believe me."

"I don't know," Susan said. "I can try."

CHAPTER TWO

AFTER ANOTHER HOUR or so of unpacking and talking, neither mentioning the idea of murder again,
sticking instead to safe subjects like boys and sex,
Colleen left to go home and help her mother pre-
pare for the cocktail party her parents were having
that afternoon. The Spencers were active members
of the Boston aristocracy, entertaining a good deal
in their tall, dignified townhouse in Louisburg
Square, the most exclusive and expensive section
of Beacon Hill. Colleen, to her never-ending embarrassment, was debuting this year and so she always had to make an appearance at her parents' affairs. They were invariably called affairs.

Actually it had always been rather a scandal to
Boston society that Colleen had gone to Baldwin
Prep School in Cambridge—a school known for
both the sciences and the performing arts—instead
of attending the Faulkner School as did most
proper young Bostonian women. But Colleen, who
wanted to be a doctor, had chosen Baldwin, a school
that drew most of its students from Cambridge,
Brookline and Newton, with just a few commuters
from Boston. As far as Susan knew, there was only
one other person who had gone on to Baldwin from
the private school she and Colleen had attended in
the Back Bay: Patrick Finnegan.

Susan sat back on her bed, thinking about Patrick. She and Colleen and Patrick had been best
friends all through elementary school, sharing

that wonderful sort of three-sided friendship where no one felt left out. Then the year that they turned thirteen, something had happened. She looked at Patrick one day and realized that he was taller, his voice was deeper and he was starting to get muscles. Maybe Patrick had noticed something too because suddenly they couldn't talk to each other anymore without blushing. They didn't arm-wrestle, they didn't tickle each other, they didn't do any of the things they had always done. It was Colleen who brought them together, persuading Susan to ask him to a Sadie Hawkins' dance, starting the romance, a romance so shy that it could scarcely be given the name.

Sometimes, in moments of completely unselfish reflection, Susan wondered if Colleen might resent the relationship, thinking it came between her friendship with Susan. Maybe she did—but probably not often. Colleen had spent her formative years in a series of crushes on football-player types. Patrick was not a football-player type. He was the star of the Baldwin soccer team and an excellent skier but he was definitely not a football-player type.

At any rate, the romance had continued. Oh, she had gone out with people in New York and she knew he had gone out with a few other girls but they had kept in touch, writing brief, awkward letters and seeing each other the few times that Susan had come up to Boston to visit. She could hardly wait to see him. As soon as the phone was put in, she would have to—

"Susan?" someone called from the door.

She looked up to see her little sister Wendy, small and grinning, wearing jeans and a faded green rugby shirt. She looked exactly the way Susan had looked when she was ten, both with the same long, dark hair and blue eyes. Their mother called the color an almost Prussian lapis lazuli.

14

But then, having worked in and bought from art galleries for years, she had always been a show-off about colors. When they were little, she and Wendy had been trained to call things carmine or magenta instead of just plain red. It was the kind of obnoxious thing that endeared one to art teachers. Art teachers had always thought that she and Wendy had great talent in spite of the fact that, as her father often remarked, they were barely capable of drawing baths.

"What is it, Wendy?" she asked, pulling out of her inner monologue.

"We're going to McDonald's. What do you want?" Wendy giggled at the still-overwhelming mess in the room. "My room's finished."

"Yeah, figures." Susan grimaced, not wanting to think about all the work she had to do. "Get me a cheeseburger and some Tab."

"They don't have Tab."

"I don't care then, something diet."

"What's the magic word?"

Susan got up, coming over to the door.

"I'm bigger than you are," she said.

"That's the magic word," Wendy agreed, escaping down the hall.

Susan followed her, meeting her father at the bottom of the stairs.

"Where did you get the sweatshirt?" he asked.

"Your drawer."

"Why don't you wear your own clothes?"

"Because," she fastened her arms around his neck, "I want to be just like you."

He grinned wryly, searching for his car keys in the pocket of his flannel shirt.

"Wendy?" he called. "Let's move it, okay?"

"Having fun unpacking, Dad?" Susan asked.

He merely grumbled and she continued past him to the kitchen, where her mother was standing on a chair, washing the shelves of the glass-doored cup-

15

boards. She wore an old black leotard, a worn and probably buttonless Oxford shirt and jeans.

"Don't tell me you can't find anything to do," her mother said, scrubbing.

"I'm just taking a break." Susan moved two boxes of dishes from a kitchen chair and sat down. "Colleen still here?"

"No, she had to go home." Susan grinned. "Her parents are having an Affair."

Her mother nodded, pushing the chair across the linoleum to start on another set of shelves.

"We were invited," she said, climbing up on the chair again.

"You going?"

"I expect not," her mother replied, scrubbing harder.

Susan watched her, the sight of so much energy making her tired.

"Mom?" she asked.

"What?" Her mother pointed to the bucket. "Put some more hot water in this for me, will you?"

Susan carried the pail over to the sink, dumping out the dirty water, then adding soap and refilling it.

"Do you think Colleen is obsessive?" She put the steaming bucket on the counter.

"She always has been. Why? She isn't on another one of those terrible diets, is she?"

"She said she wasn't."

"She's not looking very healthy."

"She's kind of tense." Susan leaned against the counter. "If she—I don't know—said she thought someone had been murdered, would you believe her?"

"Would you?"

"I don't know," Susan shrugged. "I mean, it's not like she lies."

"She has a pretty overactive imagination." Mrs. McAllister smiled, moving down to another set of

16

shelves. "Not that you're any slouch in that department." She laughed. "I should never have let you watch the Mod Squad."

"I guess."

"Has she mentioned any of this to her parents? Or the police?"

"I don't know."

Her mother turned to look at her, her cloth dripping soapy water.

"I guess they kind of think she's nuts," Susan admitted.

"Obsessive even?"

"Yeah," Susan agreed reluctantly.

"You know," her mother rinsed her cloth. "You two would have been wonderful on the Warren Commission."

"I bet we would have figured it out."

Her mother laughed.

"I bet we would have."

"Maybe you could get Colleen to focus her energies on that?" her mother suggested cheerfully.

"Yeah." Susan pushed away from the counter. "I'll tell her you said so. You need help or anything?"

"Don't put yourself out. What do I care if I have to do this *all by myself*?"

Susan sighed, opening a box of dishes.

It was after their lunch of lukewarm McDonald's that the doorbell rang.

"I'll get it!" Susan shouted, just passing the door on the way upstairs to work on her room. She shoved her sweatshirt sleeves up to her elbows, then opened the door just in time to catch Patrick checking his reflection in the glass at the side of the door.

He straightened up, flushing. "Uh, hi," he said.

"Hi." She also flushed, realizing that she must look awful, running a quick hand through her hair.

17

"I mean hello." She moved forward and they hugged stiffly.

"I, uh . . ." He put his hands in his pockets. "I would have called only—"

"Only we don't have a phone yet."

"Yeah."

"They're putting it in now."

"Yeah?"

She nodded, gesturing for him to come in. She closed the door and they stood awkwardly in the hall. He was even taller than he had been in the summer, she noticed; taller, with the thick black hair combed to perfection, his eyes the greyish-green she had always found so attractive. He had on grey corduroys, a darker grey crewneck sweater and a white Oxford shirt, with a blue CB ski jacket over that and the scarf she had given him for Christmas.

"Been skiing a lot?" She gestured toward the row of tags on his zipper.

"Pretty much." He unzipped and zipped the jacket once. "Nice apartment."

"Yeah."

"Looks a lot bigger than your old one."

"Yeah." She pushed up her left sleeve. "Uh, come on in."

He followed her into the living room and they sat down on the couch, several feet apart.

"So," Susan said.

"Well," he agreed.

"I'm sorry I look so awful. It's just—well, we've been unpacking and—"

"I think you look cute."

"You do?"

His eyes went down.

"I sure do," he said. They smiled at each other, Patrick moving closer. "How's your family?"

"Cranky. How's yours?"

"Okay. My nephew grew a tooth."

18

"He must look very handsome."

"Yeah."

"How's your father?"

"I don't know," he shrugged. "Okay, I guess. He wants me to fly out for spring vacation."

"Are you going to?"

"Probably. I think he just wants me to meet his new girlfriend." He smiled, touching her arm. "You really look great, Susan."

"I think you do too." She moved her hand to take his. "Can I ask you something?"

"Absolutely."

"Was Colleen kidding about someone being murdered at your school—*our* school?" she corrected herself.

"Oh, God, that." He fell back against the couch. "She sure didn't waste any time." He shook his head. "Susan, you of all people should know better than to believe her."

"Why shouldn't I believe her?" Susan tried not to sound as defensive as she felt.

"She gets kind of carried away." He grinned. "You both do."

"Is that patronizing?"

"No. It's accurate." He moved some stray hair out of her face. "What are you doing tonight?"

"I have a date."

"Yeah? With who?"

"You don't know him."

He laughed, his hand brushing her cheek.

"What would happen," he brought his head closer to hers, "if I showed up around seven-thirty?"

"I would look ravishing and you'd take me to a movie."

"What if," he kissed her, "I showed up around six-thirty?"

"I'd look ravishing and you'd take me to dinner."

19

Blairsville High School Library

"And a movie?"

"Yeah."

"What if," he kissed her again, "I show up around six-thirty? Sound good?"

"It sounds great," she said.

CHAPTER THREE

It was the next night, Sunday night, and Susan was hanging up posters in her room while Colleen went through her closet to see if she had any interesting clothes.

"I like this." Susan stepped back, nodding at the full-length Humphrey Bogart poster that Colleen had brought over for a housewarming present. "You have very good taste."

"You don't." Colleen held out a purple and yellow Hawaiian shirt. "Tell me you don't wear this."

Susan grinned.

"And these?" Colleen held up a pair of purple ballet slippers with laces more than long enough to snake up and around a calf.

"With a purple LaCoste, don't worry." Susan grinned again, unrolling her Woody Allen poster and looking for the best place to hang it. "What is Boston, a cultural vacuum?"

"You tell me." Colleen lifted a misshapen clay bowl from Susan's desk. "I see you still have this."

"Yeah." Susan looked at it fondly.

"I always hated it," Colleen shuddered, putting it down. "I could never figure out why you painted it this color."

"Yours came out uglier."

"It did, didn't it?" Colleen read the label on a bottle of darkly amber perfume, then lifted her eyebrows. "Sultry Tigress?"

"I like it." Susan blushed.

Colleen sprayed a little, pretended to choke, and recapped the bottle.

"Tell me about the tea today," Susan changed the subject.

"Oh, that." Colleen winced. "It was really a drag."

"Were you well-behaved?"

"I was a delight." Colleen grimaced. "The girls and I—we call each other the girls, it's friendly-like—are just having *ever* so much fun getting to know one another."

Susan laughed at her friend's perfectly mimicking tone.

"It was just fab, you know?" Colleen went on. "I mean really fab. Simply *everyone* was there."

"Yeah? Like who?"

"Well," Colleen thought. "Allison Bixley-Baines was there. Allie is just so much fun. And Leila Winchester. Leila's a scream, just a scream. And Melissa Prendergast, of course. You simply *can't* have a party without Melissa Prendergast. They call her Muffy for short, isn't that cute?"

"You're really a bitch, you know that?" Susan grinned.

"Yes," Colleen gave her a condescending nod. "Anyway, I said to Mummy, 'Mummy,' I said—"

"Enough already, I get the point." Susan shook her head. "How do you put up with them?"

"I just sit there and eat. The food's always really great." Colleen laughed. "I told them I had an intestinal condition."

"What did they say?"

"They thought I was vulgar."

"You are."

They both laughed.

"So," Colleen sat down on Susan's desk. "You nervous about school tomorrow?"

"I'm terrified. It's even worse having to start in the middle of the year."

"Don't worry, it's an okay place. You'll like it."

"Murderers and all?"

Colleen's expression stiffened and she slid off the desk, crossing to the bookcase, her back straight.

"I'm sorry," Susan said after a brief silence. "That was a pretty jerky thing to say."

"It sure was."

"Well, I'm sorry."

"Terrific," Colleen nodded. "You're sorry."

"Well, I am. My God, Colleen, I was only—"

"Hey, look," Colleen cut her off. "What do I care if you don't listen? So what if no one listens? You think I care if no one listens?"

"Yes."

"Well, I don't. As far as I'm concerned, you can all—" She stopped, pressing her arm against her eyes, her hand a tight, trembling fist.

"But you don't care," Susan said quietly.

"Am I crazy?" Colleen asked just as quietly, her eyes brighter than normal. "I'm so sure it's murder." She turned. "Susan, can I at least show you? You'll have to go to the school for a couple of days to understand but then can I show you? If you think I'm crazy, I'll forget about it, I really will. I just need to show someone."

"Show me what?"

"The way they all are. The way the whole drug thing is. I don't know, everything. Okay?"

Susan nodded. She played with the section of her Top-Sider sole that was beginning to crack, then looked up.

"Colleen," she put both feet on the floor. "What if it really *was* murder. Should you be fooling around with it?"

"Oh," Colleen brushed that aside. "I'm being careful."

"Yeah, but—"

"Look, don't worry about it. I'm not stupid." She managed a smile. "Let's just forget about it for a

23

while. I'm tired of thinking about it. What are you wearing tomorrow?"

"My purple Hawaiian shirt."

"Right." Colleen's grin was genuine this time. "Patrick will love it."

"Hey." Susan sat back against the headboard, relaxing. "While we're on the subject, what are the guys like at Baldwin?"

"Other than Patrick?"

"Yeah. I know *him*."

"Well." Colleen sat on the desk again. "There's Jon."

"He's the one on the wrestling team?"

"Yeah." Colleen pretended to flex her muscles. "What a body."

"Does he know you're alive?"

"Yeah. He thinks I'm a grind." She looked up. "If you say I am, I'm going to hit you."

"I didn't say anything."

"You didn't get a chance." She frowned, thinking. "Anthony's kind of—" She glanced at the Humphrey Bogart poster. "No, he's not your type. Maybe Lance, you'd probably love Lance."

"I don't think I want to hear about Lance."

"Believe me, you don't," Colleen agreed.

"Hi!" Wendy bounced in in her Lanz nightgown. "Am I interrupting?"

"Yes," Susan said.

"Susan!" Colleen smiled at Wendy. "You're not interrupting."

"What are you talking about?" She sat down in Susan's desk chair, her arms fastening around her knees.

"Men," Susan said.

"Again?" Wendy looked less enthusiastic. "That's all you ever talk about."

"No, it isn't." Susan grinned. "Sometimes we talk about sex."

24

"And sometimes we interrelate the two topics," Colleen nodded solemnly.

"Sex?" Wendy perked up. "Tell me everything!"

"We don't know everything," Colleen said.

"What *do* you know?"

Colleen and Susan looked at each other.

"You're better off picking it up on the streets," Susan said.

"Hey." Wendy's shrug was supposed to be sophisticated. "It's not so much. I mean, I read *Forever.*"

"You did?" Colleen frowned at her. "What are you doing reading *Forever*?"

"You were reading *The Happy Hooker*," Susan pointed out.

"That's different."

"Why is it different?"

"Look," Colleen turned back to Wendy. "Don't read *The Happy Hooker*, okay? It's really boring."

"Okay, I won't," Wendy said, the lie bright in her eyes.

"Anyway," Colleen changed the subject, "how do you feel about going back to your old school tomorrow?"

"I can't wait!" Wendy's eyes were eager now. "Can you wait, Susan?"

"Yes," Susan said.

While eating breakfast the next morning—that is, pretending to eat breakfast—Susan was even less enthusiastic about the thought of school, starting to get nervous about it. Wendy, chic in her kilt and sweater, was in a wonderful mood, chattering away about how much fun it was going to be, about how much she loved school and wasn't Susan excited? Her mother, who also looked chic, was in a great mood because after she took Wendy to school, she was going up to Newberry Street to meet with the owner of the Norton Gallery and talk about resuming her old job. Her father was in a good mood be-

25

cause after he dropped Susan off at Baldwin, he was
going to his advertising agency for his first day as
vice-president. Susan, who felt neither chic nor
cheerful, grumbled and drank orange juice.

The phone rang and she jumped up, grateful for an
excuse to forget breakfast.

"I've got it." She lifted the receiver. "Hello?"

"H–hel—" The faint voice broke off.

Susan frowned and hung up.

"Who was that?" Mr. McAllister pushed Barnaby,
one of their two Siamese cats, off his briefcase.

"Wrong number, I guess." Susan frowned into the
mirror.

"Oh, look at the time." Mrs. McAllister stood up,
finishing her tea. "Come on, you'd all better get moving." She paused, sniffing. "New perfume, Susan?"

Susan flushed.

The drive to the prep school in Cambridge was
much shorter than she would have liked, having
been praying for hours of traffic on Storrow Drive
and even more hours of traffic on Mass Ave. Both
roads were reasonably clear and as they got closer to
the school, she began to feel sick to her stomach.

"Dad," she swallowed, "I don't want to go. I really
don't want to."

"You're going to be fine." Mr. McAllister swung
the car into a parking place, frowning at the ambulance and milling crowd in front of the main entrance. "I wonder what's going on."

"Maybe someone's stuck in that phone booth."
Susan craned her neck to see more, climbing out of
the car. She caught sight of a limp figure on the
ground. They approached the quietly buzzing crowd,
a group mainly of students with a few teachers
standing by.

One of the paramedics rose, shaking his head at a
man who stood in the front. Susan recognized him as
the headmaster, whom she had met when she had
had her interview for admission to the school.

26

The crowd shifted at the paramedic's report, buzzing more loudly, and Susan saw the face then, the vacant eyes, of the body on the ground just before another paramedic pulled up the sheet to cover the body. It was Colleen.

CHAPTER FOUR

"DRUGS," someone muttered. "Who would've believed it?"

"I would," someone else said. "She's been really weird lately."

"Colleen Spencer," the first person said. "Who would've believed it?"

Susan stared at the stretcher, at the paramedics lifting the sheeted shape, at the sheeted, unmoving shape being carried to the ambulance. She watched, but the whole scene seemed far too awful to be real.

"Susan." Her father had one hand on her shoulder, the other on her back, each very gentle. "Go get in the car, okay? I'll be right there."

She didn't move, numbed in that long moment before pain first hits.

"Go on." The hand on her shoulder came up to the back of her head and he held her for a second. "I'll be right there."

She walked to the car, conscious of every step, of the effort it took to move her legs and the effort it took to use her arms and open the car door. She climbed into the front seat, closing the door, watching the ambulance pull away, red lights flashing silently. Then the lights changed into her father, crossing through her line of vision on his way to the car.

He opened the door, lowering himself into the driver's seat, not moving for a few seconds.

"Susan, I—" He reached over and took her hand. "I'm so sorry."

She didn't answer but just clutched his hand, hanging on to it with both of hers, hanging on as he backed out of the parking place, as he pulled away from the school, hanging on all the way home.

"I'll be in in a minute," she said as he parked in a space one building down from their apartment.

He nodded, squeezing her hand and then getting out of the car.

She sank lower in the seat, fastening her arms across her chest, staring through the windshield at Beacon Hill with all its hundreds of memories. Red brick townhouses, cast-iron lamplights, steep and narrow red brick streets—she closed her eyes, afraid to let herself think.

Colleen. Colleen Hamilton Spencer. Her best friend in the whole world. In her whole life. Someone she had always depended on, someone who had always been there, someone—special. Someone very, very special.

She closed her eyes even more tightly, trying not to see that vacant, pain-stiffened expression and the small, fist-curled hand the sheet hadn't quite hidden. Dead? How could she be dead? Last night they had been joking about *The Happy Hooker* and now this morning—? Last night they had been talking about the tea, about Humphrey Bogart, about purple Hawaiian shirts. And about murder. They had talked about murder.

Susan sat up straight, realizing for the first time what should have occurred to her immediately. Murder. Colleen had been murdered! She didn't take drugs, she had never taken drugs. So she had been murdered. She must have been.

But what if she had changed? a small voice asked from somewhere deep inside her head. You hadn't seen each other in three years. She had been so thin, so jumpy, losing her temper too quickly—she had changed. She had changed a lot. It could have been drugs. It could easily have been drugs. How else would she have known so much about—no, never! Susan shook her head, wondering how she could even think like this. How could she even think at all?

She sat there for a long time, the cold physically numbing, yet soothing. A car door slammed and she looked out at the street to see a taxi pull away and her mother cross to the sidewalk. They saw each other at the same time and as her mother came toward the car, Susan scrambled out, suddenly needing her desperately.

"Mom," her voice choked, hurting against her throat. "Colleen—"

Her mother nodded, putting her arms around her, and Susan leaned against the steadying warmth, trembling from the cold and the shock, her heart pounding in her chest and her ears.

"Come on," her mother said, her arms tightening around Susan's back. "Let's go inside."

Susan nodded, letting her mother guide her into the house and to the living room, where she sank onto the couch, exhausted. She stayed hunched there for what could have been hours or minutes, letting her mother help her off with her jacket at one point, taking off her sweater a little bit later, then deciding she was cold and putting it back on.

It was still later, maybe morning, maybe afternoon, when her mother came in, carrying a tray holding a sandwich and a glass of milk.

"Why don't you eat this?" She put the tray on the coffee table.

"Thanks, but—" Susan pushed the food away. "I'm not hungry. It looks good though."

"You might want it later." Mrs. McAllister sat down, putting her arm around Susan's shoulders. "Is there anything I can do?"

Susan shook her head.

"I love you, you know."

Susan nodded, hunching her shoulders.

30

"Does it help?"

"I guess."

They sat there for a while, not speaking. The doorbell rang and her mother stood up to answer it, returning with Patrick, who was pale and expressionless and had obviously been crying. Upon seeing Susan, he almost started again.

"Susan, I can't believe it," his voice shook. "I—"

She took his hand as he lowered himself onto the couch, his eyes dark and wide with bewilderment.

"She—I just can't believe it. I talked to her right before she—" He gulped, trying to keep the tears in check, his hand gripping hers more tightly. "We had Calculus and she didn't show up and I couldn't figure out why she—and then we heard sirens and everyone ran outside and she—" He stopped, his hand squeezing hers so hard that she nearly winced.

"How did it happen?" she asked, almost whispering. "Did they find out who did it?"

"What?"

"Who did it. Did they find out who did it?"

He stared at her and then let out a long breath, releasing her hand and leaning forward, his arms on his knees.

"Did they find out?" Susan asked again, afraid from his reaction to hear the answer.

"Yeah," he said. "Did they find out."

"What? Patrick, come on!"

"The police," his expression was stiff, "said that it was either an accidental overdose or suicide."

"What?" She felt a tightening in her chest and throat, a tightening and a choking.

"They said there's been some bad stuff around the city lately and she might have gotten some that was cut with strychnine or something."

"But that would be—"

"They're investigating, but everyone seems pretty sure that it was either an accident or—"

31

"But she didn't take drugs," Susan interrupted before he could say the second word again.

This time his face crumpled and he turned away, his hand covering his eyes.

"They searched her locker, Susan," he said, his voice shaking. "Trent and everyone did. It was full of stuff."

"What do you mean?"

"Ludes, coke, everything. And the teachers talked about how weird she'd been acting and the police said it looked like a classic case and—" He turned away even farther, hiding his face.

"But she never—"

"What do you know about it? You've been gone for three years!"

"What do *you* know about it?"

"I don't know." His voice was very small. "Except she's been acting really weird. I mean like obsessed. That guy Peter who died—that was an accident, I swear it was. But she kept talking about it, about drugs and murder—people thought she was going crazy."

"Wait a minute," Susan shook her head. "This is Colleen, remember? Our best friend, remember?"

"Yeah," he said bitterly. "Best friend. She sure cared a lot about us, didn't she?"

Susan flinched. He noticed and took her hand again.

"I'm sorry," he said. "I didn't mean to—"

"Would you mind leaving?" She jerked her hand free. "I want to be by myself."

He started to speak, then nodded, touching her shoulder in a brief caress before standing up.

"Can I, uh," he swallowed, "call you later?"

"Yeah."

"Okay." He went to the door, not looking back.

She stood up and walked over to the window, watching Patrick zip his jacket and start down the hill, his shoulders hunched against the wind and

32

just-starting snow. It always snowed a lot in Boston and many of her memories were of snow. In fact, she had met Colleen in the snow.

One day when Susan was in the second grade at the elementary school on Marlboro Street, the second– and third-graders were outdoors at recess and they decided to have a snowball fight, breaking into noisy teams and creating forts out of snowbanks, packing hard balls of ammunition. Susan was dragging a huge chunk of snow over to her fort when a loose snowball hit her in the head, knocking her down. She scrambled up, furious.

"Hey!" She tried to see who had thrown it since the rules were that no one would start the fight until the forts were finished.

Colleen Spencer, a girl who was in her math group and always got all the right answers, was standing about ten feet away in a blue ski suit, a bedraggled hat clinging to long, blond hair as though it were frozen to her head. She was flushed from the cold and out of breath.

"Sorry," she said.

"You hit me! That's against the rules!"

"Sorry."

"Yeah, well, it's against the rules," Susan said again, grumpily.

"Yeah, *well*, I'm sorry."

Susan brushed the snow off her clothes, climbing over the drifts to resume work on her fort, deciding that she really couldn't stand Colleen Spencer. But Colleen had followed her, either not noticing or not caring that Susan was angry.

"I'm sorry I hit you," she said.

Susan didn't answer and Colleen lagged behind, about to return to her own fort. Susan waited until she was walking away, then bent down, gathering up a handful of snow and packing it hard into damp mittens. She spun around and threw it, catching Colleen in the left ear, knocking off her hat. Colleen fell

33

but was up instantly, hurling a large handful back. Susan ducked and it hit a boy behind her.

Then it was war. The entire second and third grades clambered over the walls of the forts, snow exploding in the air, the piles of ammunition rapidly going down. Most of the kids went after Colleen since she seemed to have started it and, grinning, she met the charge. The rest came for Susan, seeing her as an accomplice. She and Colleen found themselves retreating together, becoming a team by necessity. They were driven back by the melee of snowballs but hurled their own with equal force, if not number. Then two of the boys turned on the pack with a devastating attack from the rear and the group went after them, laughing and shrieking across the playground.

Susan struggled to her feet, half-buried by snow, as Colleen searched for her hat, both of them laughing.

"Sorry I hit you," Susan said.

They had been best friends ever since.

CHAPTER FIVE

THE POLICE and coroner's reports were both prompt and precise. The coroner's report talked about a "drug-induced allergy trauma" and a "lethal dosage of an altered lysergic acid diethylamide compound." In other words, bad LSD. The police said that they had conducted a thorough investigation and found no reason to suspect foul play, pointing to the pattern of the victim's recent tension and paranoia, probably caused by exposure to undue stress and misuse of narcotic substances. An unfortunate tragedy, they called it.

The papers jumped on the story, apparently loving the drama of it all: society girl, outstanding student and projected valedictorian of her senior class, an Early Decision admittee to the Brown medical program, a model teenager in every way. And then they made it sordid. Sordid and scandalous and sensational. They turned the "unfortunate tragedy" into a story about a scheming deceitful girl who had a secret and serious drug addiction and printed a photograph of a tall, beautiful, All-American debutante.

Susan didn't finish any of the articles. She cut them out carefully and put them in a box in her desk drawer in case she wanted to look at them someday, which she knew she wouldn't. Ever.

The funeral was scheduled for Thursday morning at ten o'clock. It was to be a simple ceremony, with only the family and a few close friends. Some closer than others.

She decided to wear her dark grey skirt and a blazer. She dressed slowly, buttoning her shirt with clumsy hands, dazed with the realization that this was the day of her best friend's funeral. She was getting dressed for her best friend's funeral, putting on her black-leather boots, brushing her hair, doing normal, everyday things; today, on this day that was anything but normal.

When she came across her purple Hawaiian shirt in the closet, she had to hold onto the door for a second. Had Colleen been with her, she would have suggested that Susan wear the shirt just to lighten the atmosphere. Susan had always loved that irreverent sense of humor.

"Susan?" her father called from the hall. "We can go whenever you're ready."

"Uh, be right there." She closed the closet with an effort and picked up her blazer. Turning to check herself in the mirror, to check to see how she was going to look at her best friend's funeral, she saw Humphrey Bogart staring at her from the poster that Colleen had brought her. She stared back at him, then went over and took the poster down. She rolled it up neatly, stood it in the corner and left the room.

The church was small and crowded, dark and quiet. She had been to only two funerals before, each of which had been for very old, very distant Irish relatives. They had been almost cheerful affairs, with loud, slightly drunken receptions afterward where everyone made jokes about what her great-aunt or whomever would have thought about all of this. What would Colleen have thought about all of this? Quiet, solemn rows of well-dressed people, well-dressed and repressed. The altar was bare except for a few elegant arrangements of white flowers and Susan knew that Colleen would have hated this, every bit of it.

She sat between her parents in a pew near the front, none of the scene seeming real to her. Looking around, she saw only a few familiar faces, all of them belonging to cousins and aunts and uncles whom she had met at the Spencers' house at one time or another. There were a lot of people her own age in the church, some of them accompanied by parents, some not, all staring straight ahead with tight expressions. Colleen's parents and her older brothers and sister were probably outside or on the way over or coming from wherever it was that the immediate family stayed.

Some people just coming in sat down across the aisle two rows back and Susan turned to see Patrick with his mother and stepfather. He looked as though he might not make it through the services. She kept staring until he glanced over and they exchanged weak nods. He was wearing a dark grey suit and she wondered how he felt. Betrayed? Hurt? Angry? All three? Or did he just feel empty? She felt empty. Absolutely empty.

Then it was starting. Colleen's family had filled the front pews, the coffin had been brought in, the minister was speaking. None of this was real, it couldn't be real. She hung on to the pew in front of her, trying not to look or listen—or feel.

"—this horrible tragedy that has snatched Colleen from us in the golden years of discovery, the joyful beginning of life—"

Susan closed her eyes. Everyone else in the church seemed so strong, so controlled. How could they listen to these words and stay controlled? She clung to the pew, feeling her father's supporting hand underneath her elbow, wondering how he had known that she needed it.

Colleen's sister was at the lectern now, giving a shaky reading, and Susan closed her eyes even more tightly, seeing and hearing an eight-years-older Colleen. Listening to the voice, the familiar pitch, the familiar inflections, she remembered a conversation they had had the summer before when Colleen had come to New York to visit her.

"If it's going to happen," Colleen had leaned forward on her elbows, sitting at the kitchen table in the apartment on East Seventy-first Street, "I figure I might as well make a big splash. I mean, I want lots of people to come."

"Well, you're going to be famous, right?" Susan, making brownies, moved the spoon vigorously through the stiffening batter.

"Yeah. You can be infamous."

"Thanks." Susan threw a chunk of batter at her.

"Delicious," Colleen said, catching and tasting it. "You'll make someone a fine little wife."

"Spoken like a true Spencer."

"That's for sure," Colleen grinned. "Anyway, one thing, if they give me an open casket—I hope my eyes are crossed!"

"That's gross."

"And I think," she took a moment, deciding, "a white, flowing gown. Sort of Gothic, you know?"

"Too dressy. I'm wearing tennis stuff." Susan hit a good backhand of dough, getting Colleen in the shoulder.

"In case you run into a game down there?"

"Who's going down?"

"Hey, if *anyone* plays a stupid organ, I'm going to wake up and scream!" Colleen leveled a finger. "I'm holding you responsible."

"What do you want, the Vienna Boys' Choir?"

"I don't know. See if you can get the Stones."

"What should I have them play?"

" 'Baby, Come Back!' " Colleen laughed and Susan joined in.

"I want 'So Long, Farewell,' " Susan decided.

"And 'Stairway to Heaven.' "

"And 'When Irish Eyes Are Smiling.' We can't forget that!"

"And 'I'm Leaving on a Jetplane!' "

They had almost fallen off their chairs with laughter.

"Just as long as there's no organ," Colleen gasped.

Susan jerked herself out of the memory, almost expected to see the coffin fly open and Colleen stand up, irritated by the way the funeral was being conducted. Instead the coffin was closed and she thought about what lay underneath the polished mahogany lid. Unexpectedly dizzy, she grabbed her mother's arm for support, her father's hand coming underneath her elbow again. The spell passed and she supported herself on the pew railing, turning to see what Patrick was doing.

He was gone and she met eyes with his mother, who gestured with her head toward the door, her expression strained. Susan turned, pulling on her mother's arm.

"I have to go outside," she whispered.

"Are you okay?" her mother whispered back.

"Patrick just left."

Her mother nodded, moving back to let her out, and Susan slipped down the side aisle, trying not to attract attention, knowing that everyone was staring at her. A funeral attendant held the door for her and she went outside, so relieved to be in the fresh air she forgot about Patrick for a second.

Then she saw him across the churchyard. He was leaning against a stone wall, his back to her. She crossed over to him, noticing the uneven running footsteps he had left in the snow.

"Pat?" She put a gentle hand on his shoulder.

He spun around, angry and startled, tears bright on his cheeks. He started to say something, then relaxed when he saw who it was.

"I didn't feel good," he said weakly.

"Neither did I." She reached up, resting her hand on his cheek, wiping at the tears. He closed his eyes, trying to control himself, covering her hand

39

with his. "It's okay," she whispered. "Don't worry."

He shook his head, crying harder.

"Here, come on." She led him over to the steps at the side exit of the church, sitting him down and putting her arm around him.

"I didn't want anyone to see me," he gulped.

She leaned over to kiss his cheek, smoothing his hair back with her free hand.

"It's like," he struggled to get control. "It's like she didn't care about any of us, like she just—" He shook his head, losing the little control he had gained, clutching her to him, his heart pounding against her chest. "I'm trying so hard not to hate her, Susan."

"I know." She rubbed his back, still gently stroking his hair with one hand.

"Do you hate her?" He looked at her, his face wet with tears. "I can't stop hating her."

"I can't stop loving her," she said quietly.

"Even though—"

"Even though. I mean," she pulled him over, "what are best friends for?"

He started to cry again and she held him closer, rocking him in her arms until they heard organ music and the church doors opened, the procession starting to file out. He broke away from her, rubbing the heel of his hand across his eyes.

"Do we have to go to the cemetery?" he asked shakily.

"Yeah."

"I, uh," he took a deep breath, "don't think I can do it."

"I need you."

He nodded then and reached over to take her hand, both of them standing up.

The graveyard ceremony was short and emotional. Susan clutched Patrick's hand during the entire service, staring at the bright flower arrangement, the

40

colors seeming out of place against the stark white snow and barren trees. When it was over, they walked toward the line of cars to wait for their parents.

"You starting school on Monday?" he asked.

"Yeah."

"I'll talk to you tonight?"

"Okay."

He kissed her forehead, then walked to his car, shoulders slouched.

Driving away from the cemetery, Susan looked back at the grave. He's right, Colleen, she thought. Why did you have to do it? How could you do it? Lysergic acid diethylamide, death resulting; no reason to suspect foul play. If only it could have been murder. I was so sure that it was murder. Then no one could be mad at you.

The morning at the school returned—again she could see the ambulance, the gawking crowd, Colleen's limp body lying just in front of the telephone booth, the forlornly swinging telephone, the telephone—

"Oh!" She jerked upright.

Startled, her parents whirled around, to look at her.

"I'm sorry," she said hastily. "I was just thinking."

They turned back, absorbed in their own thoughts.

Murder. It *had* been murder, she knew it had been murder. But now she was sure. The telephone swinging! Right before she and her father had left the house that morning the phone had rung and a person had started to say hello. She had assumed that it was a wrong number. But what if the call had been from Colleen, trying to get help? Somehow she had managed to dial Susan's number, knowing that Susan was the only one who would understand. But she hadn't had a chance to—

Colleen, I'm sorry, she apologized inwardly. I

41

thought, I really thought—the stuff in your locker, the police, the coroner—I thought— She shook her head, barely able to believe any of this. It was murder. Her best friend really had been murdered.

The car slowed and she glanced up, stunned to see that they were home.

"Susan," her father turned around in the front seat. "Are you sure you still want to go to Baldwin? If you'd rather, we could—"

Not go to Baldwin? She had to go to Baldwin.

"I'd rather," she said, managing to snap out of her thoughts enough to speak. "I mean, Patrick's there and—"

"Are you sure?" her mother asked.

"Very." She *had* to go to Baldwin. She climbed out of the car, fired with a new determination. She was going to go to that school and find out who had killed her best friend!

CHAPTER SIX

WHAT SHE NEEDED now was a plan, a calm, rational plan. Where to start, what to do, how to do it. What she couldn't do was tell her parents. Any time she had tried to bring up the idea of murder, they had been very gentle, very understanding and very discouraging. All they wanted was for her to forget the whole thing and try to get over it. Murder was a word no one wanted to hear.

Besides, how could you tell your parents that you were going to investigate a murder? When you got right down to it, the phone call wasn't really all that conclusive. The police would probably call it a coincidence or say that Colleen was calling for help in the terror that she was overdosing. It would make sense to them—of course the girl would call her best friend. As they said, they had no reason to suspect foul play. So she couldn't go to the police. And how could she tell her parents about a murder they were quite sure had never taken place? Even if she could convince them, would they allow her to get involved?

The other problem was Patrick. First of all, she knew that he didn't even want to *hear* the word murder. And if she did tell him and he believed her, what could he do? Everyone knew that he had been one of Colleen's closest friends. All that he would accomplish would be to make people suspicious, which was the last thing she wanted. The one thing she had on her side was her anonymity: No one in the school knew her or her background except Patrick and the

43

headmaster, Mr. Trent. Oh, other people would find out—Patrick would introduce her around and certainly the teachers would know, but for the most part she would simply appear to be a new girl from New York whose father had been transferred to Boston. Unless she went around telling people, no one could connect her with Colleen. And that was her ace.

After all, there had been a murder. She had to keep remembering that there had *actually* been a murder. To find out what had happened, she was going to have to cultivate every single person in Baldwin who had ever had anything to do with drugs. And if people were trying to cover up a murder, how much luck would Colleen Spencer's best friend have in getting answers to questions? But as a new kid from Manhattan who suddenly found herself in Boston and was maybe looking for new drug connections, she might have some luck.

What she needed was enough room to be able to move without interference. This meant that Patrick, particularly the romantic aspect of their relationship, was going to be in the way. Unless—unless she included him in the deception. No matter how careful she was, there was always the danger that people might learn about her friendship with Colleen and she would have to be prepared for that. People who had been at the funeral might recognize her. The solution wasn't perfect but she could probably get away with it. She had, after all, been gone for three years. If Colleen had changed, why couldn't she have changed too? Maybe she had gotten into drugs as well. That way it would be more of a coincidence that she had known Colleen, a coincidence rather than a problem. She could convince Patrick about the drugs without too much difficulty, maybe even convince him that she had known about Colleen's "habit" all along. It would be a lousy thing to do to him but she

44

could always explain everything to him after it was over. If it was ever over.

So that was the plan. She would be the new kid from New York—slightly hostile about having to move and enter this new school—smart, tough and looking to make some connections. And if she had to alienate Patrick along the way, if she had to alienate *anyone*, she would. Right now the important thing— the only thing—was to find out what had happened to her best friend.

Sitting in her English class on Monday morning, she tried to keep her mind on the lecture her teacher, Mrs. Brenner, was giving about some of the more abstract facets of existentialism. Colleen would have loved it.

She glanced down at her new book, *The Stranger*, then around at the people in the class, weakly returning Patrick's grin of welcome.

"So, what do you think?" he asked, walking over when class had ended.

"Of the school or the class?"

"Both."

A blond, ruggedly handsome boy passed them on his way to the hall.

"Hey, Finnegan, making time already?" he asked, his grin arrogant and with a touch of a sneer. "C'mon, give the rest of us a chance!" He winked at Susan.

"You'll have to be faster," Patrick said, smiling stiffly.

"That'll be easy." He grinned at Susan, his teeth white and straight, and headed toward the hall.

After he was gone, Susan kept her eyes down, knowing that she wouldn't be able to resist smiling when she saw Patrick's undoubtedly furious expression.

"Who's he?" she asked.

"Tim Connors." Patrick scowled at the door,

clenching his fist. "He's such a—uh, what do you think of him?"

"Think of him? I don't even know him."

"He's really a jerk." Patrick hit his right fist into his left hand. "He thinks everyone's in love with him because he's got muscles."

"I like your muscles," Susan said.

He grumbled but she could tell that he was pleased.

"Come on." He took her books out of her arms. "These don't look too heavy. I'll carry them down to your French class for you."

Going into the cafeteria for lunch, she had her first moment of sheer panic, knowing that Patrick had a different lunch period. She stared at a room full of blurred, unfamiliar faces and gripped her lunchbag, trying to decide whether or not to just skip the meal.

"Well, hi there."

She turned to see Tim Connors grinning at her, his reddish-blond hair shining in the artificial light, very muscular, very tall and very handsome in the style of the classic lifeguard.

"Looking for anyone?" He flashed the grin, his chest expanding in a deep breath that she suspected was intentional.

"N–no."

"One thing for Finnegan, he has good taste." Tim's eyes moved up and down. "Very good taste." The grin widened.

Susan flushed and looked away, embarrassed by the quick scrutiny.

"I'm Tim Connors." He held out a strong hand.

"I'm Susan McAllister."

"Hi," he said and she was relieved to see that he didn't recognize the name. He grinned, finally releasing her hand. "Sitting with anyone, Susan?"

"Not exactly," she admitted.

"Come on then. I'll introduce you to some people."
He gestured across the crowded room.

He walked behind her and, very aware of his eyes watching every move she made, Susan slowed her pace, moving until she was walking next to him instead of a few feet ahead. He pointed to a table in the back and she felt the knot of tension in her stomach grow, knowing that she wasn't going to be able to eat.

Come on, she told herself. You're supposed to seem confident. You're supposed to seem as though Baldwin is a little provincial for your tastes. You have a reputation to make.

"You guys, this is Susan McAllister." Tim pulled out a chair for her. "Randy, Paula, Beverly and Alan. You get all of that?"

"Sure." Susan opened her lunchbag, embarrassed again as one of the boys elbowed the other and then grinned at Tim. One of the girls frowned at the boys while the other girl stared at Susan, her apple poised in mid-air.

"Have we met before?" she asked. "You look familiar."

"I don't know." Susan busied herself with her sandwich. "You ever been to Manhattan?"

"Not really. I guess you just look like this girl who used to go to my old school." The girl, Beverly, shrugged and bit into her apple.

"What was your old school?" Susan asked, keeping her voice casual.

"Longfellow. It's in the city."

Longfellow. My God, I *did* go to her old school! How come I don't remember her? The place wasn't *that* big.

"Longfellow, huh?" she said aloud. "Sorry, I've been at Patterson."

"Yeah?" Randy or Alan, she couldn't remember which was which, leaned forward. "You know Lori Carson?"

47

"I think so. She was a couple of years ahead of me."

"My cousin," he nodded. "She always said it was a pretty wild place."

"It is," Susan agreed. "It's a lot of fun."

"How come you moved?" the other girl, Paula, a bit chunky with limp blond hair and wire-framed glasses, asked.

"Oh, that." Susan made her expression just irritated and glum enough to be convincing. "My father got transferred."

"You didn't want to come?" Tim asked.

"They didn't bother asking," she said, wondering how her parents would feel about that character assassination.

"Well, cheer up." Tim gave her the grin, which she decided was probably sexy *because* of the arrogance. "Maybe you'll end up liking it here."

"Maybe," she said.

When the bell finally rang, she looked down at her almost untouched food, then slowly put it back in the lunchbag, crumpling it up.

"You don't eat much, do you?" Tim asked.

"Guess I'm kind of nervous today," she managed to smile.

"You could use the weight." His eyes moved with her as she stood up. "You a dancer or something?"

"I did some gymnastics at my old school."

"You look it," he nodded, also standing.

"I bet you play football, right?"

"Yeah." His chest expanded again. "Baseball and wrestling too."

"And I bet you've got all the moves, right?" she asked, wondering whether he had any idea how transparent he was.

He just grinned and she shook her head, going up to the trash can to get rid of her lunchbag.

"Hey," he caught up to her. "Maybe we can get to-

gether sometime." He glanced at the clock as the
warning bell rang. "Like this weekend?"

"Maybe," she agreed.

"Sounds good." He rested a possessive hand on her
arm but she didn't move, not wanting to antagonize
him. "See you later."

"Yeah," she said.

She spent the rest of the day watching people,
looking for something, anything, in anyone, that
might suggest drugs. This place seemed so clean-cut
and upstanding, all button-downs and headbands. In
New York it was easier to know about people—the
way they dressed told a lot. Here it was different.
She found herself being suspicious of the few people
in torn jeans or Army jackets just because they were
different. She was going to have to figure out some
better way of making contacts than by relying on ap-
pearances.

She stood at her locker after school, taking a long
time with her books. She packed them slowly into
her knapsack, feeling very depressed and very lonely. She couldn't remember having felt lonely before,
really lonely. She knew the feeling now. All around
her people were talking and laughing, making noisy
plans for whatever they were going to do after
school, that night, the next weekend. How could they
be so cheerful when Colleen had only been dead for a
week? She knew that Colleen had had friends, lots of
friends, because the funeral had been so crowded.
Also, she had been the class treasurer, a position she
hadn't won just because she was good at math.

In Calculus and History, Susan had noticed that a
few people had looked at her kind of funny when she
took the empty seat and she realized, with an un-
pleasant stomach-twisting, whose seat it probably
had been. But other than those brief moments, it was
almost as though Colleen had never existed, as
though the school was pretending that none of it had

49

ever happened. It didn't seem right, it didn't seem real.

She turned around, seeing that the hall was just about empty, except for a couple of girls wandering out of the Girls' Lav. They were dressed in tight sweaters, tight jeans and Candies, unlike most of the other people at Baldwin, who looked about as conservative as you could get. She decided to take a chance and start something. When you looked at people around the eyes, you could sometimes get a feeling about drugs and these two looked to be more likely candidates than anyone else she had seen.

Not taking time to consider all the possibilities of the impulse, she strode down the hall, looking for the nearest water fountain. She found one and paused, listening for their footsteps. When they were just about to round the corner, she bent over the fountain, making it appear as though she were taking a pill.

"Didn't you ever hear of looking both ways?" someone behind her asked.

"Huh?" Susan glanced up, startled, and saw Tim's friend, Beverly, a few feet away. She started to choke from swallowing too fast and took a quick gulp of water. "I was just thirsty."

"Right." Beverly leaned back, hands going into the pockets of her wide-wale corduroys, her eyes amused.

The two girls whose attention Susan had originally planned to get had passed now, neither of them even pausing. Her face red, Susan bent to drink again.

"You know," Beverly said, "you're going to have to do better than that if you want to get away with it around here."

"Get away with what?"

"Hey, look, save it for your parents." Beverly sounded bored, fluffing up her thick brown hair with one hand. "Can I ask you what it was?"

50

"Allergies," Susan replied, moving just a trifle off balance, remembering that the pill was supposed to be taking an effect. "I've got allergies."

"Right. Jesus!" Beverly shook her head. "You must really think we're stupid at this school."

"I have to go," Susan said, her face feeling hot.

"Yeah, sure."

Susan started down the hall, walking with a slight stilt to her steps.

"Hey," Beverly said after her.

"What?"

"That way goes right by the office."

"Yeah," Susan turned to look at her, trying to sound bored. "So?"

"I'm willing to bet you can't maintain. Wouldn't you be better off going the other way?"

"Hey," Susan shrugged. "Don't worry, I can handle it."

"Who's worried?"

They looked at each other for a long minute, neither speaking, Beverly's eyes calm and quietly challenging. It occurred to Susan that Beverly wasn't the kind of person you would want to have for an enemy, that she would be a formidable opponent.

"Yeah, well," Susan broke the gaze. "Thanks for the advice." She turned and walked toward the office.

CHAPTER SEVEN

AFTER DINNER that night she found herself sitting in the living room with Patrick, trying to catch up with some of her new classes.

"So, do you understand this?" He glanced at her over his calculus book.

"What?" She tried to find her place on the page. "Oh, of course."

"Well, it's important—it's integration! We've got a test coming up on Friday."

"I know." She focused on the page. None of it made any sense. "I'm sorry, I can't—I don't know."

"Yeah." He shut the book. "I know what you mean." He took a deep breath and let it out. "You think it'll ever be any easier?"

"I don't know." She picked up his hand, studying the bones, studying the vein that was going to stick out when he was older. "Pat?"

"What?"

"Where do you think she got it?"

"Got what?"

"You know."

"Oh, God." He sat back, closing his eyes. "Tell me you're not going to start talking murder. I can't go through that again."

"I'm not," she lied. "I just wonder. Don't you?"

"I don't know. I don't even want to think about it."

She didn't say anything for a minute, caressing his hand, tracing the vein with her fingers.

"Do you think it was from someone at school?" she asked.

"I don't know." He sounded tired. "Probably."

"Who?"

"Susan, I'm telling you, I don't know! It could have been a lot of people."

"Like who?"

He let his breath out through clenched teeth, staring at the ceiling.

"What does it matter?" he asked. "You really have to know all the details? She's dead—isn't that enough for you?"

More than enough. "I just wondered," she said.

"Yeah, I know."

"Who deals?"

"How would I know?" he asked. "It's not like I run around buying drugs all over the place." He looked at her. "Yeah, I know, you just wondered." He turned his hand over so that he could look at hers. "You've got such small hands. They always freak me out."

She nodded, moving closer to him.

"Oh, God, I don't know," he sighed. "Vince Parker."

"Is he the one with the Army jacket?"

"Huh?" Patrick tilted his head. "Oh, no, that's Mike Cohen. He's into individualism."

So much for stereotypes. "Which one is Vince?" she asked.

"Tall guy with glasses. Looks like a real Poindexter. He's in our calculus class."

"*He's* a dealer?" Susan asked.

"So I hear. I don't think he sells much more than pot though." He closed his eyes, thinking. "Charlie Schwartz. Burt Wilson. They're both juniors." He opened his eyes again. "I'm telling you, I really don't know. There's a lot of people you could probably get pot or ludes or something from. And maybe Schwartz could get you coke. But LSD? God, Susan, when was

53

the last time you heard of anyone selling LSD? That's sixties' stuff. I mean, you know how it is. Mostly people just drink at parties."

"Yeah. So where'd she get it?"

"I don't know. There must be someone around selling it, but whoever he is, he's good. I can't figure it out. Maybe I don't want to figure it out," he added more quietly, touching the scar on her left hand, gained in the fifth grade when she and Colleen had been playing on a fire escape and she had fallen off, breaking her wrist and cutting her hand on some glass. "Susan?"

"What?"

"Did you ever try it?"

"What, you mean pot?"

He nodded.

"Yeah," she said. "Did you?"

"Yeah. Did you like it?"

"Not really," she shook her head. "I tried it a couple of times and I just got dizzy."

"You were probably hyperventilating.

"Probably," she agreed. "I lost my depth perception too. It really gave me the creeps, if you want to know. What about you?"

"I didn't really like it either." He lifted his arm around her. "I don't know, they say you have to smoke a few times before you get high but it never seemed worth the trouble, you know?"

"Yeah." She leaned against his shoulder, noticing the Polo insignia on his shirt, feeling the warmth from his chest through the cloth. "You know that girl Beverly? She's in a couple of our classes."

"Yeah, what about her?" He bent his head down, grazing her hair with his lips.

"What's her last name?"

"Johnson." He kissed the tip of her ear, nuzzling his way down to the lobe. "Don't you remember her? She went to Longfellow."

"Really? I don't remember."

"Sure you do." He kissed her neck. "She came right before you left. Moved here from Manchester or some place."

"I really don't remember." Susan frowned.

"Well, maybe it was just as you were leaving. I forget."

"What's she like?"

"She's okay. Kind of a bitch though." His lips moved up her neck to her jawline. "She used to go out with that guy Connors."

"Really?" She turned to look at him.

"Yeah. They were going out for a long time. Then they broke up and he was going out with Priscilla Gardiner and she started seeing his best friend Randy." His lips traveled up to her cheek, then down toward her mouth. "Kind of bitchy, huh?"

"Why? I mean if they'd broken up already."

"I don't know. I just never got the feeling she liked Randy much." He kissed her. "She's pretty wild."

"Really? She doesn't look it."

"Well, she is." He kissed her again, then pulled away. "You going to kiss me back or what?"

"Oh, right." She put her arms up on his shoulders. "I'm sorry."

"Hey, don't do me any favors."

"Patrick." She pushed her hands through his hair, watching it fall back in place, moving her hand to the back of his neck and bringing his head over to hers. "You're a really good kisser," she said against his mouth.

"Yeah?"

"Yeah. You been practicing?"

He laughed. "No." His hands drifted around her waist. "Have you?"

They laughed, sliding closer together, using their eyes to grin at each other as they kissed, then closing them, still kissing, both breathing more quickly.

Hearing a sudden giggle, Susan drew back, sighing and resting her head on his shoulder.

55

"What is it?" he murmured. "Something wrong?"

"Company."

"Huh?" He turned and she could feel him sigh too.

"Sorry," Wendy said, giggling again.

"Wendy." Susan lifted her head. "If you don't get out of here, I'm going to break your legs."

"I'm hungry, it's not my fault. I have to go to the kitchen." She pointed to the door at the far side of the living room, then giggled once more. "Hi, Patrick."

"Hi," he said.

" 'Bye," Wendy said and hurried her way through the room to the kitchen.

"Hey." Patrick kept his voice low. "It's getting late. You want to walk me to my car?"

"You're *leaving*?"

"I'm scared to go out there by myself."

"Oh. If you want, I could call my father," she suggested, playing innocent.

"I'm scared of your father."

Susan laughed, kissed him, and went to get her coat.

She stood at her locker before English the next morning, worrying about the homework she hadn't done the night before.

"Hey, hi." Tim came up behind her. "How are you?"

"Okay. How are you?"

"Not bad." His eyes went down over her, then he touched the sleeve of her sweater. "Nice."

"Thank you." She focused her attention on her locker, embarrassed. Why did guys always have to do that? Colleen had a theory that if you checked them right back, pausing to stare, they would be too embarrassed to do it to you again. But this guy would probably love it.

"Hi, Tim," a svelte blond girl said as she walked

by, tossing her head so that her hair rippled over her shoulders and down her back.

"Hi." The girl with her also flipped her hair back, although somewhat less successfully.

"Hi," he said, his tone neither encouraging nor discouraging.

"Lots of women, huh?" Susan closed her locker.

"Juniors," he shrugged. "Who wants juniors?"

"What, freshmen more your style?"

His eyes wandered down her figure, pausing all the way. "No," he said, his gaze staying at her chest.

She scowled, moving past him and down the hall.

"Hey," he came after her. "I'm sorry. That was a pretty jerky thing to do."

"Yeah, it was," she nodded.

"Well, I'm sorry." He put on his grin. "You mad at me?"

I bet he's used that grin to get himself out of trouble his entire life, she thought. "It was a jerky thing to do," she said.

"I said I was sorry." He touched her arm, running his hand down her sleeve. "I think you're cute—is that so bad?"

Susan extricated her arm from his hand.

"You going to English?" he asked.

She nodded, letting him walk down the hall with her, deciding that it was still too early to antagonize anyone. He took the desk on her left, making a big production out of pulling her chair back for her.

Patrick came into class just as the bell was ringing, smiling as he saw her and heading over to sit next to her. The smile faded when he noticed Tim and he stopped, taking a seat in the back. Susan winced as he avoided her eyes, a slight red flush of either anger or jealousy starting in his cheeks.

"Hey, you okay?" Tim asked.

She nodded, focusing her attention on the front of the room and the teacher, Mrs. Brenner. She took out her copy of *The Stranger*, opening to the right page and bending over it, hoping that she would at least *look* as though she were paying attention. When the dismissal bell rang, Tim stood up, every muscle in his shoulders and back rippling as he stretched.

"Good old French," he grimaced. "You coming?"

"Well, I—" She saw Patrick heading over. "I'll probably see you there."

"I'll save you a seat." He walked to the door, shoving Patrick out of his way.

Patrick pushed him back, then continued over to Susan's desk. "Why were you talking to him?" he demanded.

"Pat, we were just—"

"I hate that guy! I don't want you talking to him!"

"Patrick, I was only—"

"Well, I don't like it!" His fists were tight. "He's a jerk."

"You're jealous."

"I am not! I just don't like him slobbering all over you, okay?"

Susan smiled at him.

"Okay," he admitted. "So maybe I'm jealous."

"I was just talking to him," she said. "Don't get worked up about it."

"I'm not worked up!"

"Okay, you're not."

"Yeah, well, look." His jaw was as tight as his fists. "If he touches you—"

"Come on, we're late." She noticed Mrs. Brenner at the front of the room, trying not to listen as she went through a lesson plan.

"I guess." He slouched out of the room after her.

Tim was standing next to the door, leaning lazily against the lockers.

"I thought I'd—" He saw Patrick and glowered. "What is this, Pat? Anything I can do, you can do better?"

"Look, you—" Patrick took a step toward him.

"We're all kind of late." Susan moved between them. "Maybe we ought to get going."

She found herself standing alone as each of the boys stormed off in a different direction, assuming that she would go with the other. She sighed, watching them leave. Maybe it wasn't worth it to try to know Tim better. She had been planning to ease up on her efforts today but Patrick had changed her mind. He had said that Beverly was "pretty wild." Maybe he meant sexually, maybe he meant a lot of things; but if Beverly was wild, it made sense that Tim probably was too, since they had gone out together. That made him worth getting to know. Worth getting Patrick angry? Definitely worth getting Patrick angry.

The warning bell rang and she started down the hall toward French class.

Later, during gym, she sat on a bench in the Girls' Locker Room, listening to everyone talking and laughing as they changed into shorts and LaCoste shirts. A couple of girls gave her tentative smiles that she tried to return, again feeling the deep loneliness that had begun the day before.

Had Colleen been in this class? It would have been so different: Colleen introducing her to friends and teachers, sitting with her in class and at lunch. She leaned forward, fumbling for her gym clothes inside the knapsack she used for her books. She held the shorts and shirt tightly with the sudden fear that she was going to cry—right here, right in front of all these people she didn't know. She gripped the shorts and shirt, her eyes shut.

"Hi."

She stiffened, then saw Beverly sitting down next to her.

"Hi." She kept her eyes lowered.

"You okay?"

"Yeah, sure."

Blairsville High School Library

"Your eyes are kind of red."

"Allergies." Susan took off her blazer.

Beverly laughed. "No kidding?" she asked.

"No kidding." Susan took off her sweater.

"Guess you managed to maintain yesterday."

"Guess I did." She unbuttoned her Oxford shirt, leaving the turtleneck.

"You wear a hell of a lot of shirts."

"It's cold up here."

"You always so friendly?"

"No."

"I think you're scared."

Susan looked at her sharply, again recognizing the fact that this girl would be a formidable opponent.

"Scared?" she asked.

"You heard me. Your parents dragged you out of your little New York cocoon, made you come to a new school—I bet you're scared to death. Hell," she shrugged, "I would be."

"You ever been to New York?"

"Not really."

"Well, I'll tell you. It's not a cocoon."

"I still think you're scared."

Susan shrugged.

"You miss your friends?"

"Yeah." Susan thought about people she'd known in New York, thought about other friends for the first time since Colleen— "Uh, yeah, we used to have a pretty wild time."

"Things can be wild up here too." Beverly's voice was defensive.

Susan almost grinned, not having meant to use the word "wild." Nothing like a good Freudian slip to lighten the atmosphere. "I guess," she said, pulling her jade alligator shirt over her head. "My friends in New York kept telling me to watch out for Pilgrims."

"You think we're Pilgrims?"

60

Susan looked at the class: laughing, enthusiastic people in bright colors and tennis sneakers.

"Kind of," she said. "Everyone looks like a Kodak commercial."

"Great." Beverly stood up, pushing her hands into the pockets of her Adidas shorts. "You dress that way too."

"Hey," Susan shrugged expansively, tying her Tretorns. "Don't want to rock the *Mayflower*."

Beverly frowned. "That's either funny or it's the stupidest thing I've heard all day," she said.

"It's funny."

Beverly kept on frowning, then let her face relax into a smile, a smile that did a great deal to change her appearance, wiping away the cynicism.

"You're right," she said. "It is." Then the frown returned. "Pilgrims, huh?"

"Hey, who knows?" Susan stood up, zipping her shorts. "I might be wrong."

"You might be," Beverly agreed.

"Pilgrims, huh?" A voice asked, maybe irritated, maybe amused, as she stood at her locker after school, getting her things ready to go home, not looking forward to fighting the buses and subways. Tim grinned at her, wearing sweatpants and a faded red and white baseball shirt. He had on jogging shorts over the sweatpants and a sweatshirt cut off at chest level over the baseball shirt, with the strange, high, sneaker-like shoes wrestlers always wore.

"What do you mean?" she asked.

"Oh, she even plays innocent," he nodded. "I heard you don't think we know how to have fun up here."

"Did I say that?" She made her smile just flirtatious enough, wondering what he meant by fun.

"The way I heard it, you did."

"Must have been someone else." She stuffed her French book into the knapsack.

61

"What's your definition of having fun?"

"What's yours?" She put in *The Stranger* too.

"Maybe they're the same."

"Maybe," she said, quietly aware that her hands were shaking and busying them on the knapsack zipper.

"Maybe we should find out."

"Maybe."

"Can I call you tonight?"

"Sure." Flirtatious, remember? Come on, you can do it—it's for a good cause. Patrick will get over it.

"You have a phone number?"

"Oh, right." She fumbled for a pen, noticing that her hands were trembling more than ever.

"Here." He handed her a pencil and an open notebook.

She wrote down the number, her hand clenched tight around the pencil.

"First couple days are kind of rough," he said.

"Kind of."

"Things'll get better."

"Yeah?"

"Count on it," he said.

CHAPTER EIGHT

AND HE did call. He called that night, he called the next night. They didn't have much to say to each other—they didn't have much in common—but that didn't seem to bother him as he kept on calling. She found out a little more about him: he was an only child; his father was a senior faculty member at Harvard Medical School; his mother was a successful and driven attorney; and neither parent was home much of the time. It didn't sound as though any of them got along very well. His parents wanted him to go to Harvard; he wanted to go to Princeton, to get out of Cambridge and never come back. His grades had been slipping this year and he figured he had probably been partying too much. With all the athletics to back up his record though, he was pretty sure his marks would be good enough.

The partying line was encouraging, giving Susan the feeling that she might not be wasting her time on him. But the more she talked to him, the more he made her nervous. It wasn't that he hated his parents—she could deal with someone who hated his parents. Instead it was as though he just didn't care either way, as though he had no feelings at all. He didn't seem to care about anything except getting out and never coming back.

As a boyfriend he would probably be nice enough, thoughtful in all the surface ways: complimenting her hair, her clothes, maybe even bringing flowers on the right occasions. But there was an absence of

. . . what? Compassion? Empathy? Maybe empathy was the right word. He said all the right things and asked most of the right questions but his attitude was almost perfunctory. He would nod and listen to her words but something about the way he did it gave her the feeling that he didn't hear anything she said. Either he kept his thoughts absolutely hidden or there just wasn't much there. He was handsome, intelligent, athletic, apparently quite wealthy—so why wasn't she interested or attracted? In a way she was more repelled than anything else and it wasn't just because of Patrick. While it was a lot because of Patrick, that wasn't the only reason. It seemed as though half the girls in school glared at her whenever Tim came near her. If there were such a thing as a crushes-per-capita average, he would win hands down—but she just didn't feel anything for him. She was just lonely, worried and exhausted.

She wasn't sure of how much longer she could keep all of this up. At first the idea of going after the murderer—or murderers—had seemed easy. She had been sure that she could pinpoint the most likely people in school without much trouble, never suspecting that it would take so long. Now she was going into the second week with nothing more to go on than the fact that Tim Connors sometimes partied too much. Half the country could be arrested on that basis.

No one at school was being particularly friendly either. She knew that it took a while for people to loosen up but it was still hard. Since she looked straight, the people who weren't didn't want to bother with her; and since she didn't act straight, the people who *were* didn't want to bother with her either. Those who seemed like the types that she might make friends with were unusually subdued. No one was putting out much of an effort to do anything. Looking around in her classes, she was noticing a lot of unhappy people. Maybe Colleen was affecting them more than she had first thought.

Worst of all, Patrick was avoiding her. He had been angry ever since the day Tim sat next to her in English. She didn't bother trying to patch things up, figuring that they were probably going to get worse before they got better. The result was that she was spending almost all of her time alone. She had never spent so much time thinking before. Her style was doing—*Colleen's* was thinking. Lately though, she didn't have much to do. Except wait. Sit around and wait for something to happen.

Tuesday night she sat on her bed, idly patting the two Siamese cats, Barnaby and Madeline, who had been very good about keeping her company. After a while she went over to the bookcase, remembering how Colleen had helped her unpack. She had been reading and re-reading a lot recently. *The Catcher in the Rye* was sticking out a little and she reached for the familiar rust-colored paperback. Not bothering to open it, she sat down on the bed again, thinking about Colleen.

Last summer Colleen had come to visit her in New York. They had been in Susan's room, catching up on everything that had happened since the last time they had seen each other. Then Colleen had fumbled around inside her suitcase, pulling out a small, rectangular-shaped package wrapped in plain brown paper. She had explained that it was an early birthday present.

"What is it?" Susan had asked, frowning at the cheap brown paper.

"Something I think you should have," Colleen had said solemnly.

Susan shrugged, yanking the paper off, her eyes widening when she saw the title.

"*The Sensuous Woman*?" she asked.

"I think you should read it." Colleen's expression was very serious.

"What do you know about it?"

"Nothing." Colleen laughed then, moved over next to her. "I thought we could both read it and I was too embarrassed to buy it for myself."

"Is it graphic?"

"I don't know. I had them wrap it at the store."

Susan glanced down again at the brown paper. "Must have been some store," she said.

"Come on, open it."

"Hmmm." Susan turned to the beginning. " 'Every female has the ability and the right to be fully sensuous,' " she read aloud. " 'But most women never learn how.' "

"See, this way we'll be prepared," Colleen said.

"You think?" Susan skimmed the page. "It says that we can transform ourselves from drab creatures into sought-after, desired, beautifully fulfilled women."

"Sounds good so far."

"Yeah, really." Susan kept reading. "It says that you can do it even if you're 'knock-kneed, flat-chested, cross-eyed and balding.' "

"Then you're all set," Colleen grinned.

"Yeah, it's you I'm worried about."

They were nearly finished with the first chapter, laughing hysterically at almost every line, when Mr. McAllister came into the room and Susan moved the book behind her.

"What's going on in here?" he asked. "All I hear is laughing."

Susan and Colleen exchanged glances, laughing harder.

"We were just reading," Susan said.

Sitting on her bed now, thinking about that afternoon, she flipped through *The Catcher in the Rye*, remembering how from that time on she and Colleen had always told Wendy that she was knock-kneed, flat-chested, cross-eyed and balding. Wendy had always taken this personally.

Her father poked his head into the room and Susan

jumped, automatically putting the book behind her.

"I'm sorry, I should have knocked," he said. He looked at her, sitting on the bed with her hands behind her back. "What are you reading?"

She took the book out, blushing. *"The Catcher in the Rye,"* she muttered.

"Racy stuff." He moved all the way into the room, glancing around, his hands in his pockets. "You ought to get your stereo set up."

"I guess."

"I could give you a hand."

"Yeah. I don't know." She put the book down and Madeline immediately stretched a sleepy paw across it. "I guess I just haven't felt like it."

"Well, we don't have to do it today." He shifted his weight. "So, how are you doing?"

"Okay. How are you?"

"Okay." He shifted his weight again. "I mailed a check in to that tennis club. Would you like to play one of these nights?"

"Sure, if you want," she shrugged without committing herself.

"Then we'll do that." He went to the door, his hands still in his pockets. "I can go get a screwdriver and we can see about that stereo."

"Yeah."

"Okay." He started to leave.

"Dad?"

He turned.

"Remember last summer when you came in my room and Colleen and I said we were reading?"

He nodded, leaning against the desk as though prepared for a confession.

"It was *The Sensuous Woman.*"

"No kidding?" He laughed. "I had my money on *The Happy Hooker.*"

"We did that in eighth grade."

"Did you learn anything?"

67

"Oh, yeah," Susan nodded, pretending to look very serious. "Lots."

"Really?" he grinned at her. "I don't think I'm going to pursue that."

She grinned back at him, having forgotten in the last few weeks how much fun she had joking around with him.

"Tell you what." He sat down next to her, putting his arm around her shoulders. "How about I give you a hand with the stereo and then we'll go downstairs and stuff our little faces with chocolate-chip ice cream? Sound good?"

"Yeah," she nodded. "It sounds good."

In French class the next day she sat between Tim and Beverly. She and Beverly had developed an aloof sort of friendship, one based on mutual animosity and respect. She had noticed that Beverly and Tim seemed to have the same sort of relationship. She couldn't help wondering what a romance between these two cold and rather distanced people would have been like.

"This class is *so* boring," Beverly yawned, ignoring the teacher, Mr. Hanson, as he chalked irregular conjugations on the board up front.

"I'll say," Susan agreed, copying down the verbs.

"I know something that might pep it up," Beverly said.

Susan looked up with the sudden nervous fear that the opening she had been waiting for was about to appear. Beverly uncurled her fingers to reveal two small pills. Susan glanced at them, then at Tim, who was concentrating on the board. She could tell from his slight grin that he knew what was going on.

"You're going to take them?" she whispered.

"You can have one." With a quick motion of her wrist, Beverly spun a pill onto Susan's desk, her expression aggressive and challenging.

Susan clapped a swift hand over it, checking to make sure that Mr. Hanson hadn't noticed.

"But it's yours," she said, covering it with both hands.

"Go ahead," Beverly urged.

Now what do I do? Susan didn't move her hands, wondering exactly what the pill was, wondering how she was going to handle this.

"Maybe I'll wait until after," she said.

"Come on, do it now. Don't be chicken." With a casual, practiced movement, Beverly slipped the other pill into her mouth. She smiled. "They didn't teach that at your old school?"

"We only had six people in a class," Susan said. "We never even tried."

"You mean you're chicken."

"Of course not," she said. She looked at the pill, checked to make sure that Mr. Hanson wasn't looking, then pretended to take it. Instead she palmed the tablet, hoping that she had looked convincing. Before she had a chance to decide what to do with it, Mr. Hanson swept down the aisle in her direction.

"Hey!" he shouted.

Susan jumped. "Wh–who, me?" she asked.

"Yes, you! What were you doing?"

"Doing?" Don't panic. Don't panic! "I–I just took my gum out, that's all." She struggled to keep her expression calm.

He scowled at her, unconvinced. "Where is it now?" he demanded.

"I–I don't know." She glanced at the floor behind her in desperation, relieved to see the accumulated small trash of several earlier classes. "I put it in a piece of paper."

Mr. Hanson moved his jaw, still scowling.

"Well, you watch yourself," he said. "You won't get away with it twice."

"I'm sorry." She tried to meet his gaze firmly, guiltlessly.

He returned to the board, watching her all the way.

Susan sat very still, trembling, her right hand clenched around the pill. Mr. Hanson frowned at her once more, then starting writing conjugations again.

"Damn," Tim said quietly, "you think fast."

"I've had plenty of practice," she said weakly, her heart thudding in her ears. "I always seem to get caught." She tried to smile at him. "I feel like such a jerk."

"No one shoved it down your throat." He was looking ahead now, seeming to pay attention. "She just wanted to see what you'd do."

"I should have waited."

"Relax," he said. "Let it take effect."

"Yeah." She clenched her hand around the pill. "I–I hope it hurries." She could feel the dampness on her face but was afraid to do anything about it, afraid to do anything that might catch Mr. Hanson's attention. She looked over at Beverly, who was taking down notes about the conjugations, grinning broadly.

"Pilgrim," Beverly said.

Susan didn't answer, instead taking a few deep breaths in an effort to stop shaking, trying to get ready for Act II: the effect of the drug. She stared at her hand for a second, at the unseen pill. How in God's name was she going to get rid of the thing?

CHAPTER NINE

SUSAN WALKED down the hall toward the cafeteria, not looking at anyone, her eyes concentrating on her books. Someone grabbed her arm, spinning her around.

"I want to talk to you," Patrick said, his expression furious.

She held the books closer.

"What the hell happened?"

"Wh–what do you mean?" she asked.

"The whole school's talking about it! About the new kid who got caught taking pills in French, only Hanson couldn't prove anything so she got away with it."

Susan was silent, too tired to defend herself.

"Damn it, Susan, what happened?"

"I got caught taking a pill in French," she said. "Or haven't you heard?"

He stared at her, the response unexpected.

"Y–you really did?" he asked.

"I really did," she answered, hurt enough by his unhesitating accusation to want to hurt him back—even though she knew it was a lousy thing to do.

He just stared at her, his eyes dark. Without speaking, he turned away and walked down the hall.

"Patrick, wait," she called, guilt replacing the hurt and anger. "I didn't—"

He broke into a near run, hurrying down the hall and away from her.

"What's going on?" Tim came up behind her. "Was that guy bothering you?"

"No."

"You sure?"

"Yes."

"Well, he'd better not. If he does, he'll answer to me." He scowled down the hall, putting a protective arm around her shoulders. "Come on, let's go to lunch."

The rest of the day was terrible. Patrick wouldn't look at her and everyone else stared, seeming to be either amused or shocked. When she walked down the hall, there were whispers everywhere. Her teachers were suspicious and disdainful or overly concerned. Her English teacher, Mrs. Brenner, even stopped her in the hall and gave her the "I-know-you've-been-having-a-difficult-time-and-if-you-need-anyone-to-talk-to—" speech. Susan hadn't responded, too tired to deal with anyone. She managed to make it through the day, somehow, wanting only to go home to her own room and lock the door behind her.

As soon as school was over, she hurried to Harvard Square, taking the Red Line subway into Boston. This time she didn't pause to wander through the stores as she had done several times on her way home. Today she knew she wouldn't find any comfort in the friendly crowds of college students who packed every store and sidewalk. Incredible to think that only a few weeks ago her biggest worry was where she was going to go to college, if in fact she got into college at all. She had applied to Brown, Williams, Yale and NYU. Colleen had wanted her to come to Brown; Susan herself had been leaning toward Williams and its theater department. Now, after the last two weeks of playing a constant, painful role— and even after all those hours of voice and acting lessons in New York—she didn't think she cared

72

whether she ever saw the inside of a theater again. She wasn't sure that she cared about anything.

She rode the subway to Park Street, climbing up and out of the busy station to Boston Common, the park at the foot of Beacon Hill, the park where Emerson and Whitman had walked, the park where so much of Boston's history lay. She walked up to the gold-domed State House, then down Beacon Street, turning up the hill and over to Chestnut Street.

Reaching inside the zippered pocket of her knapsack for her key, she unlocked the door and went into the apartment, relieved to know that no one was going to be home. Her father was at work, her mother would be at the gallery, Wendy's school didn't get out until three-fifteen. Murdoch, whom she knew she had been ignoring lately, came racing out to the hall to greet her, his stumpy tail waving furiously.

Without pausing to take off her jacket or lower her knapsack, she scooped him up, holding him in both arms, letting him lick her face.

"Today was so awful," she told him. "You have no idea how awful today was." She cuddled him closer, starting up the stairs.

"Susan?" her mother called from the kitchen.

She stiffened, her first reaction a cold fear.

"Susan, is that you?"

"Uh, yeah," she answered, knowing why her mother was home. The school had called her. Of course the school would have called her.

"Could you come in here for a minute?"

She took a deep breath, put Murdoch down and walked to the kitchen, trying to seem casual. Her mother was sitting at the table, her hands wrapped around a mug of tea.

"Hi," Susan managed to smile. "You're home early." She looked inside the refrigerator, taking out a carton of milk. "We're almost out of milk," she remarked, pouring herself a glassful.

"You want to tell me about it, Susan?" her mother asked quietly.

"About what?" She turned, putting on a smile that her mother did not return. She took a deep breath, looking down at the milk in her glass. "You got a phone call, huh?"

"I certainly did."

"Yeah, well," Susan shrugged. "It isn't true."

"Your headmaster seemed pretty convinced."

"My headmaster wasn't even there."

Her mother folded her arms, looking small and worried rather than angry.

She isn't even going to yell at me, Susan thought, watching her. They never yell at me anymore. All they do is look worried. And hurt. She looks really hurt. What am I going to tell her? The truth won't work. If I start to talk about murder again, they're going to put me into a home or something.

"Susan," her mother said, "your father and I know that you've been having—"

"Hey, I don't care if you don't believe me," Susan interrupted, not sure of what her mother was going to say and wanting to change the subject. "What did Trent tell you? He didn't even see what happened. My French teacher's just—"

"Your French teacher isn't the only one who's spoken to him."

"H–he isn't?" Susan asked, trying to figure out who else would have and why.

"Almost all of your teachers have," her mother said, thereby answering her first question. "They say you haven't been paying attention, haven't been taking notes—" She paused. "Why didn't you tell me you flunked your calculus test?"

"I forgot."

"You forgot," her mother nodded. "Susan, you're a straight–A—"

Susan tuned her voice out for a minute, trying to figure out how to handle this. She hadn't been study-

74

ing or paying attention; they were right about that. Just because she had always gotten As didn't mean that she had to keep on getting them. Right now she didn't have time.

"—someplace else," her mother finished.

"What?" Susan looked up.

"Your father and Mr. Trent and I think that you might be better off at another school," her mother repeated herself. "In spite of Patrick. It was a mistake to let you—"

"Don't I get asked about any of this?" Susan asked. She couldn't leave Baldwin. She'd never solve the murder if she did. "You can't just shove me into another school like that. I want to stay at Baldwin."

"Susan, it would be a lot easier on—"

"On who?" Susan asked, cutting her off. "Me? Or you and Dad?"

"On all of us," her mother said.

"Yeah, well, I'm not going to—"

"Hi," Wendy said cheerfully, coming into the kitchen and banging her Metropolitan Museum of Art bookbag on the table. "How come you're home, Mom?"

"I got off a little early," Mrs. McAllister told her.

"Oh." Then Wendy grinned. "Guess what? Wait, wait, let me show you. Look!" She dragged a piece of paper out of a battered textbook. "I got a hundred in math! Susan, look."

"That's good," Susan nodded, making her way to the door while her mother examined the paper.

"Susan, I haven't finished talking to you," she said.

"Yeah, well, I already told you everything I have to say." Susan picked up her knapsack, leaving the room.

No one bothered her for a couple of hours and she lay on her bed, rereading *The Great Gatsby*, too tired to think about what she was going to do about this new problem. One or both of her parents would come in soon and she would have to deal with the whole thing but she wasn't going to think about it until then.

At a little past five there was a knock on the door. "Who is it?"

"May I come in?" her mother asked.

Susan grabbed her calculus book from the bedside table, propping it open on her knees.

"Yeah," she said.

Her mother came in, closing the door behind her, walking over to Susan's desk and leaning against it.

"What are you doing?" she asked.

"Homework." Susan indicated the book.

"Having trouble with it?"

"No."

Her mother nodded, looking around the room.

"We have to do something about this wallpaper," she said. "Maybe we can pick some out this weekend."

Susan shrugged.

"Patrick hasn't been around much lately. Is he okay?"

"We had a fight," Susan said.

"Serious?"

"Yeah."

"Do you want to talk about it?"

"Not particularly."

Crossing to the bed, her mother sat down next to her.

"All I want to do is help," she said.

"I know."

"I wish you'd talk to me."

"About what?"

"About everything—today, Colleen, all of it." She went on as Susan shrugged, idly flipping pages in her calculus book, "Come on, Susan. We've never had trouble talking."

"There's nothing to say."

"I think there is. Maybe you could start with how you feel."

"I feel fine."

Her mother reached out and touched her cheek, brushing a few strands of hair away from her face.

"Well, I do."

"I don't think you're letting yourself feel it."

Susan shrugged again, slouching over her math book.

"It would help if you'd cry."

Susan turned more pages in the book.

"Are you angry at her?"

"What?" Susan looked up. "No."

"Not at all?"

"No."

"Then how do you feel?"

"I told you. Fine."

"Susan, come on."

"I don't know what you want to hear."

"All I want is for you to—" Her mother stopped, turning to look at her. "Are you up to something?"

"What do you mean?" Susan didn't look at her.

"You are, aren't you?"

"I don't know what you mean."

"Yes, you do. Susan," her mother moved closer, "you have to accept what happened."

"I know."

"What happened?"

"She took drugs."

"And you really believe that?"

"Yeah. I mean, the police and everyone—"

"The police," her mother nodded. She pulled Susan over, holding her tight. "You think she was killed, don't you?"

"No."

"Of course you do. If I were seventeen, I would too." Her mother sighed, moving so that they were both leaning against the headboard. "Think about it." Her voice was gentle. "If there was *any* doubt in

77

*any*one's mind, particularly the Spencers', do you really think they would have closed the investigation?"

"They might."

"Trust me, they wouldn't have." Mrs. McAllister hugged her even closer. "Susan, think about it. The Spencers are very influential people."

"The Spencers are people who don't like scandals."

"It's a little different when your own child is involved," her mother said and Susan heard the double meaning in the statement.

"I don't know," she said.

"Well, take my word for it." Her mother shifted her position slightly. "Susan, I know how hard all of this has been for you. I know how you felt about her—how all of us felt about her—but you have to believe me when I say that it was an accident. It really was."

"I didn't say it wasn't."

"I know you didn't *say* it." Mrs. McAllister kissed the top of her head. "Try to remember the special parts of your friendship. There were so many."

Susan nodded.

"Do you think," her mother kept her arm around her, "that you might feel better at another school? Someplace where you could start fresh?"

"No."

"Can we at least look at some other places? Take a few tours, get you some interviews?"

Susan didn't answer, knowing that her mother was telling, not asking.

"Susan?"

"Do we have to?" she asked finally.

"I think it would be a good idea."

"Does that mean I'm going to have to go to one of them?"

"We'll see, okay?"

In other words, probably—which means that now I'm going to have to work even faster.

"Okay?" her mother asked again.

Susan nodded. She was going to have to work *a lot* faster.

CHAPTER TEN

"HEY, HI," Tim said, catching up to her in the hall the next morning, his jacket swinging open.

"Oh, hi."

"Wait, let me take that." He lifted her knapsack onto his shoulder. "You okay? You look kind of tired."

Okay, back into the act, remember? "Yeah." Susan put on a wry smile. "Trent called my parents about what happened yesterday."

"Figures Hanson would run right to him," Tim nodded. "You get in trouble?"

"Kind of." She stopped at her locker. "It was mostly the 'where-did-we-go-wrong?' speech."

"Oh, Christ," he shook his head, handing her the knapsack. "I hate that one."

"You've gotten it?"

"Twice a week." He grinned. "Since I was three."

"Rough life."

"Yeah." He helped her off with her ski jacket, leaving his hands on her shoulders. "Hey, uh, you doing anything after school?"

Maybe something's finally going to happen. "No, not really," she said.

"Randy and those guys are coming over—I don't have practice today. Thought you might want to come too."

"Sounds good," she agreed, wishing he would let go of her shoulders. "Only I'll have to call my mother and check."

"Well, try and talk her into it." He slid his hand down her arm to her wrist. "It'll be fun."

"I'll try." She looked at his hand, aware that she was getting herself into something potentially complicated. "They're threatening Catholic school."

"Yeah?" His hand took hers. "You don't seem the nun type."

Potentially *very* complicated, she decided. "I don't know," she said. "I guess it depends on your definition."

He grinned at her. "Guess it does," he said.

"You should really come today," Beverly said as she, Susan and Tim walked down the hall toward their Current Issues class. Beverly had been much friendlier since French the day before, almost as though Susan had passed some kind of test. "You look like you need it."

"Yeah," Susan agreed. "I don't know, I'll have to try to get through to my mother at lunchtime."

"It's going to be a good time," Tim said, winking at her as he held the door.

Susan tried to smile, not returning the wink. Stepping into the room, she looked for Patrick and saw him up near the front as she sat down. He looked at her, started in her direction, then saw Tim and stopped. He glowered at her, taking a seat as far up front as possible.

"What a jerk." Tim's expression was smug. "Can never face it when he gets beat out."

"What about baseball captain?" Beverly asked. "He beat you out then."

"Peace, Bev," Tim said shortly. "Okay?"

"Oh, yes, sir," she nodded. "Anything you say, Timothy."

Susan looked at her, then at Tim, and was glad that she was sitting between them. Beverly was gazing at the ceiling with a small, complacent smile while Tim scowled at his notebook.

Not wanting any part in that, Susan glanced at Patrick, who was sitting tense in his chair, gripping his left fist with his right hand. The tips of his ears were red and she knew that his face would be too. A girl sitting next to him said something to him and he turned, expressionless. When he saw Susan watching, he started an animated conversation. Susan felt a hard flash of jealousy as the girl put a comforting hand on his.

When class finally ended, Patrick shoved past her without speaking, walking with the girl. Susan sighed, piling her books together and standing up to walk with Tim.

She called her mother at the gallery to ask if it would be okay for her to stay after school and go to a drama club meeting. She didn't feel very good about lying but her mother probably wouldn't be too thrilled by the idea of Susan's spending the afternoon at some guy's house, especially when her parents hadn't even met him. Mrs. McAllister was enthusiastic, however, about a play rehearsal and said that it was fine as long as Susan was home by five o'clock. Susan promised she would be.

Beverly waited for her until she got off the phone and they walked down the hall toward one of the side exits, pausing at Beverly's locker.

"You know . . ." Susan checked her knapsack to make sure she had all the right books. "Could I ask you something?"

"Depends on what it is," Beverly said, squinting at the books on her locker shelf. "Do we have French homework?"

"Yeah. The exercises at the end of the chapter."

Beverly grimaced, taking the book down.

"Did you and Tim use to go out?" Susan asked.

"Yeah."

"How long?"

"Pretty long." Beverly took out her copy of *The Stranger.*

"Why'd you break up? I mean, if it's any of my business."

"It's none of your business." Beverly put on her coat and scarf.

"Well," Susan frowned at her knapsack, trying to figure out a way to get a better response. "Is there something really wrong with him or did you just not get along?"

"Didn't you hear me say it's none of your business?" Beverly closed the locker.

"Oh," Susan looked up. "Did you say that?"

Beverly laughed and zipped up her jacket.

"Look," Susan grinned too, "I just want to know if there's anything I should know in advance."

"Like what?"

"I don't know. Whatever."

"He's ambitious."

"So?"

"I'm just telling you that he's ambitious," Beverly shrugged. "Come on, they're waiting for us."

"Is that all you're going to tell me?"

"Yeah." Beverly started down the hall.

"You don't still like him or anything, do you?" Susan followed her. "I mean, does it bother you that we might be going to get involved?"

"Why would it?"

"I don't know." Susan zipped up her jacket as Beverly pushed the outside door open. "I just thought it might."

"Well, it doesn't," Beverly said.

"You sure?"

"Don't push me, okay, Susan?" Beverly looked at her with the hard expression, then strode across the parking lot.

Susan followed more slowly. All of this was getting complicated.

It was decided that Tim and Susan would go first,

83

the others following in Alan's battered station wagon. Tim had a Porsche.

"Nice car," Susan said.

"You like it?" Tim beamed at her, brushing his hand along the shiny red hood. "I spend a lot of time on this machine."

"I can imagine."

Tim started the car, swerving out of the parking lot, tires squealing, and Susan watched the speedometer leap from zero to fifty.

"It has great pick-up," he said.

"Yeah." Susan braced a nervous hand against the dashboard. "I noticed."

He drove deep into the Cambridge residential section, pulling into a long driveway on Brattle Street and parking in front of a large white house with black shutters.

"Your parents aren't home?" She followed him up the snow-covered front steps.

"I told you they weren't around much. Better things to do, you know?" He unlocked the door.

"Does it bother you?" she asked as they walked up a long, sweeping staircase with a well-polished banister.

"Hell, no. Keeps them out of my way." He turned onto another staircase, going up to the third floor. "Come on, I've practically got my own apartment." He grinned wryly. "Keeps me out of *their* way." He took the last two steps in a jump. "The maid used to live up here."

They passed a bedroom, dark and mysterious in various shades of green, and then a bathroom done in navy blue.

"Here." He opened a door at the end of the hall. "You can wait in here. I'll only be a minute."

Susan nodded, wandering into the room.

"Be right back." He left the room, reappearing a few seconds later. "You into coke?"

"I think I'll take it easy today," she said. "My parents'll be on the lookout when I get home."

"Whatever," he said, leaving again.

Susan unzipped her jacket and looked around the room. It was bigger than the bedroom, with light blue walls and a darker blue shag carpet. There were several large beanbag chairs and two low sofas. The walls were covered with posters ranging from the Boston Red Sox to the Grateful Dead to a picture of Reagan that someone had used as a dartboard. A stereo with huge speakers rested underneath the window, a long shelf of records next to it, another shelf of still more records by the far wall.

"You want a beer or something while I'm at it?" he asked from the doorway. "I've got some in the kitchen."

"Uh, sure," she answered. "If you're having one."

He nodded. A minute later he came in with two Molsons in one hand, a small plastic bag of marijuana and a few things that she couldn't really see in the other.

"Thank you," she said, taking the beer.

He grinned, putting his bottle on the floor and sitting down on one of the couches. He took out some rolling papers, deftly pouring an even line of marijuana on one and then uncapping a small pill bottle that he had brought in with him. He hesitated.

"You don't want to get too messed up, huh?" he asked.

"Not really."

He nodded, rolled the joint and handed it to her. She watched him make another, sprinkling some white powder from the pill bottle over the marijuana before rolling it up.

"Angel dust?" she asked, hoping it wasn't a stupid question.

"Yeah. You done it?"

"A couple of times," she nodded.

"You like it?"

85

"It's okay." She took a sip of beer, watching him roll three more joints, sprinkling some of the white powder on each, then putting the little container in his pocket.

"Tim, you up there?" Randy bellowed from downstairs.

"Yeah," Tim called back. "C'mon up."

Then the room was filled with noise and laughter as the other four trooped in, uproarious enough to indicate that they had stopped for a smoke or something on the way over. Susan stayed by the window, tensely gripping the beer bottle and the joint.

"Hey, good buddy." Randy slapped Tim on the back. "Howsabout that coke?"

Tim reached into a pocket other than the one he had put the angel dust in and took out a small silver container, handing it to him.

"Thanks, pal," Randy grinned at him. "I owe you."

Tim nodded as though he had heard that before.

"These dusted?" Alan asked, pointing to the four joints on the couch.

Tim nodded. "Anyone else want a beer?" he asked, picking up his empty bottle.

"Yeah," Randy said and then draped an arm around Beverly's shoulders. "How about you?"

"Sure," she answered.

"I hate beer," Paula complained. "It's so sour."

What's she doing here? Susan wondered. She doesn't seem to fit in with the rest of them. Paula was one of those earnest, not-very-attractive types who want desperately to belong. She and Alan were always making out all over the halls at school.

In fact, the more she looked, the stranger the group seemed. They were all so clean-cut. It make her think of those "Do-you-know-where-your-children-are?" commercials. They looked like they had parents who would only laugh at the question. But the more she looked, the less she liked them.

Paula must drive Beverly crazy, she decided as Paula shrieked and giggled when Alan pulled her onto his lap, putting one of the joints to her mouth. Alan was kind of annoying too. He was the kind of guy who made constant sexual innuendos and looked as though he might grab you when you walked by.

Randy came swaggering back, all muscles and dark curly hair. He gave Beverly her beer, then joined Tim at the stereo. Randy was a cocky, arrogant jock—naturally he and Tim got along.

"So," Beverly wandered over. "What do you think?"

"I'm impressed," Susan said, gesturing with the joint in her left hand at Alan and Paula, at the container Randy was still holding. "I didn't think he'd have these kinds of resources."

"What did you think?"

"I don't know," Susan shrugged. "Guess I didn't."

Beverly sat down in one of the beanbag chairs, kicking off her shoes. "Randy, come on." She sounded very irritated. "Not that damn Fleetwood Mac album again."

"They come out with another one, I'll play that," he said, putting the record on.

"Is Tim always this generous?" Susan asked, wanting to steer her back to the subject.

"What do you think?" Beverly asked. "Randy, how about the B-52's? Let's hear something different for a change."

"I like Fleetwood Mac," he said stubbornly.

"Oh, for Christ's sakes!" Tim reached around him and grabbed a record from the shelf. "So we hear the B-52's for once."

"I'm serious," Susan said, still trying for an answer. "Is it always like this?"

"Look." Beverly stood up, expelling an irritated breath. "Pump someone else, okay? You want to know so damn much, ask him."

87

"I wasn't pumping you," Susan said quickly. "I was just curious."

"Yeah, right," Beverly nodded. "You're always curious."

"I'm sorry. I didn't know it was such a big deal."

"Who said it was a big deal?"

"I don't know," Susan said. "I got the feeling you did."

"Why don't you just bug Tim?" Beverly asked. "Leave me out of it."

"Yeah," Susan shrugged. "Sure. Don't get so defensive."

Beverly didn't respond but strode across the room and said something to Randy. He grinned, handing her the container of cocaine and following her to a beanbag chair, large enough to hold both of them.

Susan took a sip of beer, thinking. Beverly wouldn't have been that defensive—unless there was something to hide.

She looked around the room: at Tim, releasing a slow cloud of smoke and handing a joint back to Alan; at Paula, giggling and obviously stoned; at Beverly, sitting close to Randy and bending her head to do a line of cocaine.

Maybe she was getting closer than she had thought.

CHAPTER ELEVEN

SOMEONE HAD turned the lights off except for a small study lamp in the corner and the stereo was turned way up. Susan was relieved by the darkness—it made it easier to pretend that she was as busy getting high as the rest of them were—without having taken anything at all. It was hot in the room.

She sat nervously on one of the couches, watching everyone else, her cheeks flushed from the heat and smoke. She had a sudden strong urge to run outside or at least to throw open a window but she repressed it, not wanting to do anything that would attract attention. The music was loud and pounding, its beat echoing through her head. She closed her eyes, hoping that it would help. Someone sat down next to her and she quickly looked up to see Tim, who was also flushed.

"Getting tired, babe?" he asked, touching her hair.

"No, thanks. I'm fine."

He smiled, moving closer, his arm going around her.

I knew this was going to happen. Now what do I do? "These get-togethers must be pretty expensive," she said aloud.

"Don't worry about it."

"Does everyone pay you back?"

"I said don't worry about it." He slid even closer and she moved back, unaccountably scared, noticing how big he was. "Come on, babe." He put his free hand on her stomach. "Relax."

"I am." Susan shifted, thinking about Patrick, uneasy about anyone else being this close to her. "It's just—"

"What's the matter?" His hand drifted down and she moved to avoid it. "Didn't you like the stuff?"

"It was fine," she nodded. "Where you get it?"

"Just picked it up. Prime, huh?"

"Yeah."

"Mmmm," he lowered his head, inhaling deeply. "You smell terrific. What kind of perfume is that?"

Susan felt herself blush.

"Hey," he said against her ear. "How about we go in the other room?"

The other room, the other room, the bedroom! Susan's eyes opened wide as she made the connection.

"N–no," she said quickly. "That's okay."

"I don't know." His hand moved suggestively. "It'd be easier."

"I'd really rather not."

"What's wrong?" He brought his hand up to her cheek. "You're so uptight."

"No, I'm not."

"Okay, you're not. Look, relax." He leaned over to kiss her and she made an effort not to stiffen, thinking about Patrick. "Come on, let's go in my room. I want to be alone with you."

"Yeah, but—"

"No one'll even notice," he said.

Looking around, she saw Alan and Paula spread all over the other couch, Randy and Beverly on the floor by the stereo, sharing another joint. It was hard to see much in the darkness but she could tell that Randy was amused by all the couch activity. Beverly's face didn't seem to have any expression at all.

"Look." Tim eased her back against the cushions,

trying to kiss her again. "If you're worried about protection, I'm all set."

"What do you mean, protection?" she asked uneasily.

He laughed, apparently finding the question quite funny, and brought his head down to kiss her.

Relax, she told herself. You're playing a part here, remember? Don't lose it.

"Tim," she lifted herself onto one elbow, a difficult move with all his weight on her. "I–I should maybe explain something."

"You don't have to explain anything, babe," he smiled down at her.

"Tim, it's just—" She shifted her head out of the way, avoiding his mouth. "I'm, uh, I'm kind of nervous about jumping into anything because I'm kind of"—she thought about Patrick, wishing that he were with her—"attached to someone. From home," she elaborated.

"Oh." Tim stopped smiling. "What the hell's that supposed to mean?"

"That I—I mean—"

"Great," he sat up, folding his arms across his chest, scowling straight ahead. "I should have figured you'd play virgin."

Susan opened her mouth to speak, then stopped, not sure what to say.

"What did you expect?" she asked finally. "It's not as if we—"

"Sure, babe, sure," he said stiffly. "Anything you say."

Great, now he's suspicious, she thought. I can't blow it before I've even asked where he gets his drugs and who sells around here and everything. I've got to do something. Academy Awards, remember?

"Tim, come on." She put a teasing, flirtatious whine in her voice. "Don't be mad."

91

"Why not?" he asked. "You get me going, then you turn virgin. Why shouldn't I be mad?"

"I didn't—"

"You think you're the only girl I could have asked today?" He turned to look at her. "I could have asked a lot of girls. But I asked you. I thought we understood each other, y'know?"

What a conceited jerk, she thought. I don't have to put up with this. "I guess neither of us understood," she said and stood up, walking over to the door.

"Wait a minute." He came after her. "Where you going?"

"Home." She picked up her jacket, carrying it out to the hall.

"Wait." He walked faster, standing between her and the stairs. "Don't do that. I don't want you to go."

"I got the feeling you didn't want me to stay either."

"But I do." He put his hands on her shoulders. "I'm not mad. I just said that. You don't have to go."

I wonder if it ever occurred to him that *I* might be the one who's angry.

"Come on." He steered her toward the bedroom. "Let's just go in here for a minute. Just to talk," he added as she hung back.

"I'd rather go back where we were."

"It's so loud in there." His hands slid around her waist. "I thought you might want to go someplace quiet."

"I'd rather go back where we were," she said again.

"Okay, okay," he nodded. "Then we'll do that. Have some more weed maybe."

Susan looked at his hands, then up at the cocky grin she was learning to hate, suddenly feeling very tired.

"Okay," she said. "I'll be in in a minute."

"What do you mean, in a minute?" he asked.

"You're not going to leave or something, are you?"

"I'm just going in there." She pointed to the bathroom.

"You sure you're not going to leave?"

"I said I wasn't."

He nodded but leaned against the wall to wait. She was too tired to argue and went into the bathroom, locking the door behind her. She put the seat down and sat on it, resting her face in her hands. She knew that she was close to crying but she was too exhausted and defeated to let the tears come.

More and more she was beginning to wonder about what she was trying to do. It seemed as though the harder she tried, the worse things got. It also became more and more tempting to quit.

She leaned back against the tank, looking up at the plaster-swirled ceiling and thinking about Colleen. She remembered her friend's infectious laugh, her wide smile. Sometimes Susan felt as though she might turn around and find Colleen standing right there. She felt as though she could go to the phone, dial that familiar number and her friend would answer. The best thing about Colleen was that she had always been there when Susan had needed her. She had been the kind of person who would drop everything, no matter when you called or why. The kind of person you couldn't ever imagine not being there.

Someone knocked on the door and Susan let out a long breath, remembering where she was and the situation awaiting her.

"I'll be right out," she said. She stood up, looking in the mirror, ignoring the dark circles under her eyes and all the weight she had lost in the past month.

"I'm going to get them, Colleen," she said quietly. "No matter who it is or how long it takes, I'm going to get them." She took a deep breath, straightened her shoulders and opened the door.

Tim was still out in the hall, waiting for her. "You okay now?" he asked.

She shrugged affirmatively, both her determination and her control back. "I have to be home at five," she said.

"Oh, yeah?" He looked at his watch. "It's four-thirty now. You going to take the T or you want a ride or something?"

"I can take the T."

"No, I'll drive you."

She shrugged and nodded, following him into the main room. Randy, still sitting by the stereo although he had his arm around Beverly now, looked up. Putting on her jacket, Susan saw Tim wink at him and make a surreptitious victory signal with his index and middle fingers. Beverly also caught the gesture and looked startled; glancing at Susan, at Tim and back at Susan. Susan blushed in spite of the fact that she was innocent and was about to say so when it occurred to her that it might not be a bad idea to let Beverly be unsure. That way Beverly might not be so quick to assume that she was a Pilgrim. And that might make Beverly loosen up and start answering some of the questions Susan kept asking.

"Watch the place, will you?" Tim asked Randy. "I'll be back later."

"Sure, pal," Randy nodded. "Don't do anything I wouldn't do."

Tim grinned.

"I have to be home by five," Susan said by way of casual explanation and Tim's grin stiffened slightly. She turned to Beverly. "See you tomorrow?"

"Whatever," Beverly said but Susan was surprised to see some concern in her expression. Beverly saw that she had noticed and the bored cynicism quickly returned.

"Well, uh, see you," Susan said and followed Tim out of the room.

In the car he hesitated before starting the engine. "You mad at me?" he asked.

"I wasn't really expecting you to be like that."

He shrugged, drumming on the steering wheel with one hand. "We going to see each other again?" he asked finally.

"I don't know," Susan answered. "Are we?" Keep him hanging, she thought. Just until you can ask him some really important questions.

"I don't know," he said. "If you want to."

"I guess we'll have to see what happens."

He nodded, still drumming, and neither spoke for a minute. Then he sighed and started the engine.

"Where do you live?" he asked.

"Beacon Hill."

"What?" He frowned at her.

"Beacon Hill," she said uneasily, hoping that it didn't give him any reason to connect her with Colleen. "Chestnut Street."

"I didn't know that," he said. "What are you doing at Baldwin?"

"It has a pretty good drama department," she shrugged. "Don't most of the kids come from Boston?"

"No, not so many." He started the engine.

"Beverly does."

"Yeah."

"Is she in the Back Bay or—?"

"Back Bay," he nodded. "On Commonwealth."

"Oh." Susan reminded herself that she was supposed to be new to Boston. "That's like, right near where I am, isn't it?"

"Kind of."

"It's so pretty around there."

"Yeah," he said.

They made stilted conversation all the way through Cambridge and over the Longfellow Bridge into the city. Finally he pulled up onto Chestnut Street, parking in front of a driveway near her building. He turned off the ignition and they sat there for a few seconds, Susan relieved that he hadn't driven through Louisburg Square. She had been going out of her way to avoid it and driving past Colleen's house now might have made her so upset that she couldn't cover up her feelings.

"Well, here we are," he said.

"Yeah." She picked up her knapsack from the floor of the car, holding it on her lap, trying to decide what strategy to use to start him talking. Unable to come up with anything better than to make him think she might still like him, she smiled at him.

"I'm sorry about the way everything happened this afternoon," she said. "See, when I left," she made up a quick name, "Rick and I weren't quite sure how to leave things and—well, it's just hard, you know?"

"What am I supposed to do? Wait for you to get over him?"

"No." She made her voice sound uncertain. "I mean, he's so far away and—"

Tim reached over and took her hand. She let him, deciding that this was finally her chance to try some questions.

"Um . . ." She focused on her knapsack. "Can I ask you something?"

"Sure."

"If I—well, see, I don't know who to ask really. I mean," she shifted, trying to figure out how to phrase this convincingly. "I don't really know anyone who—see, I brought some stuff from New York with me, right? Only it kind of isn't lasting as long as I thought it was going to. If I needed to, you know, get some more, who would I go to? I thought you might know."

"What kind of stuff?"

"I don't know. Coke, ludes, whatever." She shifted again. "I really need it."

"I could get you whatever you want," he shrugged.

"No, I don't want you to do it for me. Just tell me who to go to. Like that guy Vince in our English class—he deals, doesn't he?"

"Minor league." Tim sounded disparaging.

"Well . . ." She tried to remember all the names Patrick had mentioned on the night she had asked him. "What about that guy—I don't remember his name—I think he's a junior. Blond hair, really skinny."

"Charlie Schwartz?"

"Yeah, that's it."

"Sounds like you've been doing some research," he grinned.

"I asked around." She swallowed. "I—I really need to know."

"Don't worry, I'll take care of it."

"No," she shook her head. "I don't want you to get involved. You could get in trouble. Just tell me who to go to."

"You're kidding, right?"

"No," she said uneasily. "What do you mean?"

"Come on, Susan." He put his arm around her. "You think I keep all that stuff around because I'm generous?"

"Wait." The implications of that took a few seconds to get through. "You mean you're—?"

"Hell, Schwartz *works* for me," he said with more than a little pride.

"Why didn't anyone I asked mention your name then?"

"No one much knows," he shrugged. "If you're careful and let guys like Schwartz take the risks, you don't get caught."

"Wow." Susan kept her eyes down, stunned by this revelation.

"Christ." He pulled her over closer. "For someone who's supposed to have been around, you sure can be stupid. I figured you knew, especially after today."

"I guess so." She kept her eyes down, not wanting

97

to meet his eyes and let him see how shocked she was. "I didn't figure you were selling anything big."

"Would I be throwing angel dust around if I weren't making one hell of a profit?"

"I guess not."

"Damn right." He nuzzled his mouth across her hair but she was still too shocked to do anything about it. "So, what do you want me to get you?"

"Can you get anything?"

"Anything," he grinned.

CHAPTER TWELVE

SUSAN MANAGED to get out of the car and into the apartment without anything more from Tim than a good-bye peck. Inside, she let her mother know that she was home, mechanically responding to questions about the drama club and then escaping to her room.

She sank onto the bed, sitting very still, aware that she was trembling badly. Anything, he had told her. I can get you *anything*. She had almost asked him if he could get LSD but had become scared at the last second, scared that she might give herself away, scared that he might say yes. Maybe he hadn't had anything to do with it—he couldn't have had anything to do with it—but he probably knew who had. When he said the word "anything," she had felt sudden fear, starting to understand for the first time what it would really be like to find the person—or persons—who had killed Colleen. It couldn't *be* Tim —she wasn't even going to let herself think that—but he had to know something about it. He would have to. He might even have supplied the—except that she wasn't going to let herself think that. If she let herself think that, she would never be able to go near him again. And she was going to have to.

She sat through dinner, her stomach too fear-twisted to eat but passing the salt, passing the milk and answering direct questions. She wanted to tell her parents and when Wendy left the table, she almost did. But her parents had apparently been waiting for the same kind of opportunity and they started

99

telling her about the research they had been doing on private schools in the area. They had appointments to see two schools in Newton and one in Belmont on Saturday morning. Susan just nodded, afraid to argue or to tell them what she had been learning since that might just make them move faster in trying to place her in another school. Right now what she needed was time.

After helping with the dishes, so tense that she kept dropping silverware, she escaped to her father's den to try to bury herself in homework. For a while the physics problems and exercises on the *plus-que-parfait* and the *passé simple* distracted her. The distraction didn't last long though and she gave up before even starting on her calculus, standing up and moving across the room to the loveseat. She slumped down into the soft cushions, thinking about Tim, about everything she had found out so far and what she was going to do next.

As she began to get closer to the answers, the thought of being alone in this was becoming more and more terrifying. There wasn't anyone to help her. Since she couldn't tell her parents and she didn't have enough evidence to go to the police or Mr. Trent or anyone else, the only person left was Patrick. Two friends of hers in New York knew about what had happened to Colleen and while they had each written a very nice letter, she couldn't call them up and tell them what was going on. Actually the only person she could have talked to and been sure of an audience was Colleen herself. In those three years apart, they had each made other friends but neither of them had made *best* friends. You only had *one* best friend.

She looked across the room at the red phone on her father's desk. If only she could call Patrick. But what could she tell him? All she would have to do would be say the name "Tim" and he would be furious. He didn't want to hear the word "murder" either. He also didn't want to hear from her. Considering all of that, it would be hard to pick up the phone and start dialing. Chances were he'd just hang up on her.

It would be nice though. Nice to talk to him, nice to hear his voice. She needed him. And she missed him.

She heard the doorbell ring faintly but didn't get up, figuring that someone else would answer it. She slouched lower into the loveseat, trying to plan what she was going to do next. Then she heard an embarrassed cough from the doorway and looked up.

"Uh, hi," Patrick said, looking uneasy, his hands in the pockets of his ski jacket.

"What are you doing here?" She sat up straight. "I mean, hi."

"I thought you might—" He moved his hands to his jeans pockets. "I mean, I thought we could—I don't know—talk."

"Uh, yeah. Sure." She moved over on the loveseat and he sat down. "I was just thinking about you," she said.

"Yeah?"

She nodded.

"Guess I, uh," he moved his jaw. "Guess I've been thinking about you too." He frowned at his jacket, unzipping it part-way.

"You want to take that off?"

"No," he shook his head. "I don't think I'm staying long."

She started to speak, then just nodded.

"So." He jiggled his knee, watching it move. "You feel like telling me what's going on?"

"You mean about what happened in French the other day?"

"About that," he nodded. "About Connors. About the play rehearsal you went to today when the school isn't even doing a stupid play right now."

"P–play rehearsal?" she asked, putting her hands together in her lap.

"Your mother told me. Wanted to know if I was in

101

the play too." He looked at her, his eyes a dark, cold grey. "You lie to your parents now too?"

"Did you," she studied the scar on her left hand, "tell them?"

"It's none of my business if you lie to them. Where were you, off with Connors?"

Susan squeezed her hands together.

"Can't you trust me?" she asked finally. "I'm only—"

"Trust you," he nodded. "Like I trusted your best friend? Like I used to trust you? Let me tell you, Susan, I'm not into trusting people much anymore."

"Patrick, I'm doing this for a reason. I'm trying to—"

"God, Susan!" He shoved an irritated fist against the loveseat. "Just cut it out, will you? You going to keep making excuses for the rest of your life? If you like him, why don't you just say so? Half the school's in love with him—you think I care if you are? He can *have* you."

"Oh," Susan swallowed. "Then, uh," she swallowed again, "why are you here?"

"I don't know." He stood up, zipping his jacket. "I really don't know."

"I thought it was maybe so you could listen to my side of it."

"I changed my mind." He paused at the door, pulling on his gloves, then turned. "You know what kind of stuff's going around school? All about the new girl who takes drugs? Doesn't that bother you?"

"Yes."

"Yeah, well, you know what they call it? They don't call it taking drugs. They call it 'pulling a Colleen Spencer.' " His voice broke. "That's what my school calls it," he said almost inaudibly. He turned away from her, bringing a hand up to cover his eyes. "Oh, God, I wasn't going to do this. Don't look at me."

"Patrick—"

"Just leave me alone, okay? Please just leave me alone." He took two deep breaths, his other hand clenched tight. "I'm sorry I came over," he said, his voice calmer. "I shouldn't have."

"Patrick, come on." Susan stood up. "Let's—"

"Just do me a favor," he interrupted her. "Leave me alone, okay? And don't—" his voice trembled, but he struggled on, "don't pull a Colleen Spencer, okay?" His shoulders flinched at his own words and he turned, leaving the room without looking back.

Patrick pointedly averted his eyes when Susan passed him the next morning arm and arm with Tim. He couldn't help but notice the expression of blind fascination in her eyes as she hung on to every word Tim said. She also seemed to be hanging on to his arm—had she taken something again? He turned and stared in spite of himself.

She stumbled a little and he saw that she was definitely off on something. He scowled as Tim kissed her good-bye in front of her classroom, then came sauntering back down the hall.

"Whatsa matter, Finnegan?" he sneered. "Jealous?"

"About *her*?" Patrick asked disparagingly. "That'll be the day."

"Yeah, you know you wanted her."

Patrick focused in at his locker, reaching up to get his books.

"You know, Connors," he said conversationally, "I didn't know you were so heavy into drugs."

"What's that supposed to mean?" Tim asked, his voice stiff.

"Everyone knows she is," Patrick shrugged. "It makes sense that you are. I mean, she's not hanging around you for your personality."

"Who says I'm hanging around her for hers?" Tim grinned.

Patrick spun around, furious, both fists clenching.

"What, you above that kind of thing, Patrick?" Tim's grin grew bigger. "You wanted her as much as I do. And let me tell you," the grin widened, "she's worth it." He paused. "Jealous now?"

"You're lying," Patrick said. "I know you're lying."

"You mean you wish I was lying." Tim leaned against the locker next to Patrick's, thoroughly enjoying himself. "Boy, was she good. I never saw a chick take her clothes off so fast."

Patrick stiffened, gripping his Latin book.

"One of those babes who keeps moaning, y'know?" Tim went on. "Course you probably don't know what I'm talking about."

Patrick didn't say a word, his fist clutching the book tighter.

"One of the best afternoons *I've* had in a while." Tim grinned at him. "Cheer up, Finnegan. With all that Latin, maybe you'll find some nice seminary that'll take you in."

Patrick dropped the book, turning and punching him hard in the mouth, knocking him back again the lockers. Tim shook his head, lifting his hand to his face. When he saw the blood on his fingers, he leaped on Patrick, both fists swinging, and they fell to the floor, struggling, exchanging hard punches.

"Hey, boys!" a voice shouted, the headmaster striding toward them. "Hey, cut it out!"

They broke apart, each breathing hard, each with tight fists.

"What's going on, boys?" Mr. Trent sounded surprised, even somewhat hurt.

Patrick spoke first. "Aw, we were just playing around," he said, giving Tim a good-natured cuff on the head. "Weren't we, Tim, old pal?"

"We sure were, Pattycakes!" Tim returned the cuff, harder.

"Tim was showing me a hold he learned in wrestling," Patrick explained, putting a playful arm

104

around Tim's shoulders in cheerful good fellowship. "It works pretty well."

"I see," Mr. Trent nodded, half-smiling. "Well, guys, don't you think you ought to get to class?"

"We're on our way, sir." Patrick started down the hall, Tim right behind.

"See about picking up some icepacks too!" Mr. Trent called after them. They didn't smile and once they were around the corner, they halted, bristling with fury.

"You stay away from me, Connors, got it?" Patrick growled.

"Yeah, you come near me again, Finnegan, and I'll—"

"I'm terrified." Patrick shoved him again and walked down the hall to the Boys' Lav to wash the blood from his nose.

"Yeah, you'd better be," Tim said.

"Don't hold your breath." Patrick kept walking.

CHAPTER THIRTEEN

"HEY." Susan stopped Tim in the hall a couple of periods later. "Where were you during Physics?"

"Didn't feel like going." He shook her hand off.

"Well, you didn't miss—" She stopped, squinting at the swelling on his face. "What happened to your mouth?"

"Shut up about my god-damned mouth!"

"I'm sorry." She blinked at the anger in his voice. "I was just asking."

"Well, don't ask again!"

"Okay." She glanced around, seeing people in the hall staring at them. "I'm sorry." She looked at Beverly, who was standing next to her, expressionless, and then back at Tim. There was something new in his eyes, something different, vindictive. "Are you all right?"

He didn't answer, shoving her impatiently out of the way and continuing down the hall. She recovered her balance, blushing as everyone nearby stared at her.

"Are you okay?" Beverly asked, looking furious.

"Uh, yeah." Susan fluttered her hand through her hair. "Wh–what did I do?"

"Nothing." Beverly scowled after him.

"Does he do that a lot?"

"Hi, Beautiful." Randy came up behind Beverly, putting his hands on her waist, pulling her back against him. "Goin' my way?"

"You'd better go talk to your friend Tim," she said, ignoring him as he tried to kiss her.

"Yeah?" Randy kept trying to nuzzle her face. "Why?"

"Because there's something the matter with him."

"Yeah?" His hands went all the way around her waist.

"Will you cut it out?" Beverly twisted free. "I'm serious!" She looked at Susan, then took Randy's arm. "Excuse me."

Susan shrugged, watching as they moved into an alcove between a row of lockers and a drinking fountain. Beverly spoke to Randy in a low, urgent voice and Randy nodded, starting down the hall in the direction that Tim had gone. Figuring that it was okay now, Susan drifted over to the water fountain.

"What's going on?" she asked.

"I don't know." Beverly was frowning, her arms tight around her books. "Come on, we'd better get going to class."

"Well, do you think it's anything bad? Like, do you think he maybe took something?"

"I said I don't know."

"Does he do this a lot?"

"I told you I don't know already!" Beverly looked around at the emptying halls as the warning bell rang. "Come on, we're late." She strode away and Susan sighed, following her.

They were almost at the classroom when Beverly stopped. "You're new," she said. "Do yourself a favor."

"What?"

"Watch out for him."

"Why?"

"Just watch out for him. He's not—" She shook her head. "Just don't trust him too much."

"Is that all you're going to say?"

"Yeah." Beverly started down the hall again.

"Wait a minute." Susan pulled her back.

Beverly looked down at her arm and Susan with-drew her hand.

"Why did you two break up?" she asked.

"Because he punched me," Beverly said, so quietly that Susan almost couldn't hear her.

"What?" Susan stared at her, horrified.

"He punched me," Beverly said, her eyes bright.

"Did he, uh," Susan shifted awkwardly, "hurt you?"

"Yeah." Beverly looked right at her. "It just didn't show much." She turned and walked up the hall to their Calculus class.

Tim went into the cafeteria, not bothering to turn on the lights. Since it was last period, no one would be coming in and he could skip class without anyone bothering him.

He sat up on a table, resting his feet on a chair, sighing deeply and propping his chin into cupped hands, facing away from the windows and the grey, snow-threatening outdoors.

"Hey," someone said from the door.

He looked up to see Randy. "Hi," he said.

"You aren't going to class?"

"No. Are you?"

"Guess not." Randy came all the way into the room, letting the door swing shut. He sat on another table, his hands stuffed into his pockets. "What's going on?"

"Got in a fight with that son-of-a-bitch Finnegan."

"What about?"

"Susan mostly. He's jealous."

"She's good-looking," Randy shrugged.

"Yeah." Tim looked up. "He said something about me being heavy into drugs."

"He did?" Randy straightened, his hands coming out of his pockets.

"I think he was bluffing. I mean," Tim rubbed the swelling at his mouth absently, "how could he

108

know? The guy barely even drinks." He glanced over at Randy. "He was just bluffing, right?"

"Jesus, I hope so."

Tim nodded and they both stared down at the floor.

"He's always been the one I've worried about," Randy said finally. "I figured if he didn't think anything about it, no one else would."

"Yeah, I know." Tim hit his right fist into his left hand a couple of times. "It was a lucky shot, that's all. He'll probably forget it. Right?" he asked less certainly.

"He'd better." Randy's voice sounded nervous.

"Oh, Christ." Tim looked at him. "Don't start getting scared on me now. He'll never figure it out. He's too pissed off at her to figure it out."

"Yeah? What if he does?"

"He won't. You didn't hear him kicking at the police report, did you? We're still okay."

"Yeah, but—"

"It's almost over," Tim said. "Don't panic on me now. We'll graduate and once our class is gone, no one will even think about it again." He grinned wryly. "It'll just be 'an unfortunate tragedy.' You know Trent and those guys—they just want the whole thing forgotten. They don't care about how it happened. Don't want their 'community contributions,' " Tim stressed the two words sarcastically, "jeopardized."

"Yeah, I guess," Randy said, his thumb pressed between his teeth, chewing on the nail.

"Like I said, don't worry. A few months," Tim demonstrated the time with a brief sweep of his hand, "and we'll never have to think about it again."

"You mean, you could *stop* thinking about it?" Randy asked. "I don't think I'll ever stop."

"Yeah, well, that's your problem, not mine."

"How could you stop thinking about it?" Randy shuddered. "The way she—"

"Shut up about it, will you?"

"Yeah, but how could you do it? How could you—"

"How could *we* do it," Tim interrupted. "You held her down, remember, buddy?"

"Yeah, but—" Randy's eyes were huge, remembering, "I didn't know it was going to kill her."

"What did you think it was going to do?"

"I don't know."

"Hey," Tim's lip curled. "You didn't have to help me."

"I was scared. She heard me talking about it too."

"You got it," Tim nodded. "Just because you didn't help me with Peter, doesn't mean you weren't involved. You knew about it."

"Yeah," Randy said bitterly. "Only because you told me. You just wanted someone you could say was an accomplice."

"No one stopped you from reporting me."

"You knew god-damned well I wasn't going to report you." Randy was up now, pacing. "We're supposed to be friends, remember?"

"You're the one who should be remembering."

"Yeah, so what are we going to do about Finnegan?"

"Watch him," Tim shrugged. "See if he starts asking questions. See if he's getting suspicious."

"And if he is?"

"Get him out of the way."

"Uh–uh," Randy shook his head. "Not me. What, are you crazy? You really think that anyone'll believe another overdose in this place?"

"I'm not talking about that," Tim said impatiently. "I said get him out of the way. Beat him up and put him in the hospital for a while. Get him from behind so he doesn't know who did it. Make him think it's for another reason—I don't know what the hell what so don't ask me. Then by the time he's back in school, he'll have forgotten all about drugs."

Randy stared at him, still shaking his head.

"Sometimes I think you're really flipping out," he said.

"Look." Tim stood up, stretching. "It's not going to get that far, so don't worry. Like I said, he was bluffing." He let his shoulders relax. "A few months. Can't you hang on for another few months? No one else knows about it."

"Bev knows," Randy's voice was low.

"What? What do you mean she knows? How could you be that stupid?"

"She guessed," Randy said defensively. "I didn't tell her."

"Damn it!" Tim hit his fist against his leg. "Couldn't you convince her out of it?"

"I couldn't help it," Randy shrugged. "She guessed. See, she knew about all the blackmail junk with Peter and—"

"Wait a minute." Tim shook his head. "How'd she know about Peter?"

Randy flushed.

"Oh, Christ, Randy." Tim sat down, letting out his breath.

"She's my girlfriend." Randy was still defensive. "I tell her things."

"Terrific," Tim nodded. "You tell her things."

"Yeah, well, how was I supposed to know you weren't going to just pay him off?"

"For the rest of my life?" Tim snorted. "Christ, you gotta be kidding. And it's not my fault Spencer couldn't mind her own business."

"Well." Randy pulled his collar out of his sweater, uneasy. "You know Bev. She won't say anything."

"Damn right she won't," Tim nodded. "Not after I talk to her."

"Do anything to Bev," Randy said quietly, "and so help me God, I'll—"

"What?" Tim asked. "Kill me? Jesus." He yawned, standing up again. "Don't worry, it'll work out. It has so far."

111

"Yeah," Randy said.

"Well, it has. Finnegan's the only one who can hurt us, right? So we watch him. And if we have to, we take care of him." He looked up. "You with me?"

"I guess I don't have a choice," Randy said.

"Yeah." Tim's smile was menacing. "Damn right you don't."

CHAPTER FOURTEEN

SUSAN COLLECTED her coat and books, feeling dazed. After that brief moment of honesty, Beverly had completely shut off. She never mentioned the subject again, barely speaking to Susan during class and hurrying off afterward. Suddenly seeing a violent side to this guy she had been thinking of as a dumb, spoiled jock was scary. And scarily suspect. There was also that quick conversation between Randy and Beverly. To them she was just the new kid from New York and they hadn't realized how incredibly suspicious they appeared in her eyes. Something was going on. And she wanted to find out what it was almost as much as she didn't want to find out.

"Hey." An arm came around her. "You mad at me?"

She stiffened, seeing Tim.

"Come on, don't be mad." He pulled her over. "I was kind of upset. I'm sorry. You mad?"

I'm more scared than mad, she thought.

"You wanna know the truth?" He leaned closer. "I wasn't thinking straight, if you know what I mean. So don't be mad, okay?"

"Okay," she said, managing a smile. Reacting in any other way would make *him* suspicious. She had to stay in the role; she had to remember to stay in the role. "Now can you tell me what happened to your mouth?"

"Got in a fight." He glanced at his watch. "I have to get to practice. I'll talk to you tonight, okay?"

She nodded and he tapped her cheek with his right hand before turning and sauntering down the hall. As soon as she was sure he was gone, she let herself slump forward, the effort of staying calm around him very difficult, one hand gripping her locker door for support.

"God, Susan." Patrick was unexpectedly behind her. "What are you taking?"

"I'm not," she answered, pushing away from the locker.

"Yeah, you are." He was angry and worried. "What is it? Some kind of speed?"

Susan sighed, leaning against the locker with her head on her arms.

"Are you okay?" Now his voice was alarmed.

"Oh, yeah," she nodded. "Super." She lifted her head just enough to look at him. "I thought you weren't speaking to me."

"Well, yeah, but—"

"Wait a minute." She turned his face to see what looked like a bruise below his eye. "What happened here?"

"Nothing," he scowled.

Something connected in her mind and the fear that had been growing in her all day increased.

"You were fighting with Tim," she said.

"I walked into a wall, okay?" He removed her hand from his face. "I need to talk to you."

"Let's go."

"What?" He blinked. "I mean, you will?"

"Let's go." She closed her locker.

They walked down the hall, almost formally, several feet apart. Susan paused in front of an empty classroom. He shrugged and they went inside, sitting down at a table in the back. Patrick leaned forward, pushing books and papers out of the way.

"I want to know what you're taking," he said.

"I want to know what you're doing fighting with Tim," she said.

114

"Well." Patrick played with the paperback cover of a Spanish workbook. "He was saying stuff about you."

"Like what?"

"I don't know." He bent and unbent the corner of the book. "Like that you slept with him."

"And you believed it?"

"I don't know." He pushed his sweater sleeves up, exposing his shirt cuffs. "Maybe you're different when you're—" He shrugged.

Susan sat back, her arms folded.

"Well, how would I know, Susan? I didn't think you were into drugs either." He hesitated. "Are you?"

"What do you think?"

"I don't know." He ran one hand through his hair, ruffling it up. It fell back into place except for his usually well-flattened cowlick. "I really don't know."

"What do you think?" She leaned over, smoothing the cowlick down.

"I don't know. I mean, I can see you changing in a couple of years but not in a couple of days." He shook his head, the cowlick popping back up. "That first night we went out when you were back, before everything, you were so—well, you weren't like this." He moved his jaw. "Is Connors into drugs?"

"What do you mean?" She tried to fix the cowlick again. "He smokes, I guess."

"That's it?"

"As far as I know."

"Oh, come on, Susan. You weren't like this before you started hanging around him, I know you weren't. Besides, how could you *like* him? He—" He stopped, pushing her hand away from his hair. "Will you cut that out?"

"Your cowlick," she said.

"Oh, God." He brought his hand up to fix it and

she had to smile at the worried gesture. He paused. "What's so damn funny?"

"Nothing." I love him, she thought. I really, really love him. I wish I could put my arms around him.

"Connors is supposed to be Joe All-American," he said. "If he were taking drugs, it would be pretty big deal."

"Why?"

"Joe Athlete? You know what Baker would do if he found out?"

"Baker?" she asked.

"The wrestling coach. He's been trying to get Tim scholarships and everything. He and Mercer both have. Football," he explained as her eyebrow lifted.

"Why's he need scholarships? His parents can afford it."

"His grades aren't so hot. Especially this year. He almost wasn't eligible for wrestling."

"I thought he did pretty well."

"He doesn't. His father went to Princeton, so he thinks he's got pull. He'll probably buy 'em a building or something just so—" Patrick took her chin in his hand, turning her head to frown into her eyes.

"What are you doing?" She tried to pull away.

"You look fine," he said. "How come a minute ago you were falling all over the hall and now you look fine?"

"I wasn't falling all over the hall." She pulled free. "I leaned against my locker. I can't lean against my locker if I want to?"

"But I was sure you were—I mean, I saw you before and you were—" His frown was more puzzled than ever. "Susan, what's going on?"

"Nothing."

"Well, then, how come—" He stopped, leaning over the table, his right hand tapping against the Spanish workbook. "Why'd you ask me to trust you the other night?"

"I didn't—"

116

"Yeah, you did. You said, 'Trust me. I'm doing this for a reason.' Why'd you say that?"

Because I made a mistake. "I don't know," she said. "I guess I was trying to let you down easy."

"Uh–uh," he shook his head. "It was more than that. You found out something about Connors, didn't you? You've been looking for people who have something to do with drugs and you found out something about Connors."

"But I didn't," she said quickly, knowing that if Patrick started to get involved, he would ruin everything—her anonymity, all her progress.

"You must have. It's the only thing that makes sense. He knows someone who sells stuff like LSD, right? And you think you can go to them and—"

"Patrick, you're completely—"

"No, I'm not. It's the only thing that makes sense. You still think it was murder and you're trying to—"

"But I'm not."

"You must be crazy," he said, ignoring her denial. "First it wasn't murder, so you're running around making a lousy reputation for yourself for nothing. Even if it was, you really think people would come right out and tell you about it? Besides, if it was, don't you know how dangerous it would be too—"

"Patrick, just be quiet," she cut him off. What she was going to have to do was to hurt his feelings so badly that he would stay away from her, Tim and all of it until she had time to figure out what was really going on. Not only would his being involved blow everything but he was right about the danger. His becoming involved could get both of them hurt—or even killed. She had started this alone and the only way she was going to make it work was by continuing alone. So she had to get him out of it, out of the way, right now.

"You want to know the truth, Patrick?" she asked. "You really want to know the truth? You want to know all of it?"

"Well, yeah," he shrugged, looking nervous.

"Why couldn't you have just accepted it? Why did you have to make me do this?" She let out a hard breath, closing her eyes. She was going to have to make it up as she went along.

"Well, tell me," he said uneasily.

"Okay." She opened her eyes. "Don't tell me I didn't try to let you off easy. First," she forced her mind to concentrate on a plausible story, "I knew about Colleen. I mean, I was her best friend so you have to figure that she told me, right? She'd been using stuff since junior year. Since I started sophomore year, I wasn't too shocked when she told me. Nothing big—pot, maybe a little coke. Just to have some fun, you know? No big deal. She was making me kind of nervous this year because she kept calling me up when she was really stoned but I figured she could handle it. She kept talking about LSD though. She really wanted to try it. That was like around Christmas, before Christmas. So I told her to wait until I got back here and we'd try it together. Only she—" Susan let her face tighten. "It was coming, Patrick. It had been coming for a long time. You know how she was—she could barely handle beer and here she was getting into all this stuff. I mean, hey, I can handle it but she—" Susan shook her head.

"I don't believe you," he said slowly.

"Look, whether you believe me or not doesn't matter," she shrugged. "You asked for the truth, I'm giving you the truth. If you want to know, she'd been flipping out for a long time. You remember summer before last when she went on 'vacation' for a month?" Susan crossed her fingers, not sure that this "anecdote" was going to be realistic.

He nodded, expressionless.

"She wasn't traveling with her parents—they put her into one of those centers, you know, like drying-out places." She checked his eyes and decided to try something a little more personal. Like Tim. "And another thing. Tim was a jerk to tell you about it but what he said was true." She paused. "I like him, Patrick. Is that so awful? I mean, God, I was fourteen when I left. Did you really think things were going to be the same? I changed. I figured you would have too." She put on a smile, still improvising. "Those times I saw you though, it was nice. It was almost as if things *hadn't* changed. I kind of liked pretending. But now—" She looked over at him, his expression making guilt twist in her throat. "Pat, I'm sorry." She touched his shoulder. "I was hoping we would kind of just drift apart and I wouldn't have to do this. Why couldn't you have just let it go?"

He didn't say anything, obviously stunned.

"Oh, Pat." She moved her hand down his arm. "Why'd you make me do this? I was hoping I'd never have to."

"What if I don't believe you?" he asked quietly.

"Of course you don't," she nodded. "You're a nice person, you always have been. Only," she paused for effect, "not all of us are, you know." She glanced over, wondering if she had maybe gone too far with that.

He folded his arms, studying her with intense grey eyes, his mouth tight.

"So Connors is into drugs?" he asked.

"What? No. Like I told you, he smokes a little, that's all."

"Well, some of those guys must be. You wouldn't hang around them if they were *straight*, would you?" His voice was sarcastic.

"They're friends of his. They're kind of boring, if you want to know."

"I don't particularly." He stood up, his fists going into his pockets. "I think you're lying, you know. Especially about Colleen."

"Patrick, figure it out. You really think the Spencers would have hushed it up if they hadn't known she was into drugs? Just because *you* didn't notice it doesn't mean no one else did." She stood up too. "You've got to grow up, Patrick. You're still in the ninth grade, you know what I mean?"

For some reason that line worked and she had to fight to keep from hugging him and apologizing as his shoulders slumped. His whole body slouched, making him seem almost fourteen for a brief, vulnerable second.

"You know," his voice was both calm and angry, "I'd tell you what I think of you, Susan, only—" he smiled bitterly—"I guess I'm too nice for that, huh?"

CHAPTER FIFTEEN

SEEING PATRICK the next day during English only made her feel guiltier and she was glad that he wasn't in her French class. It wasn't just that he wouldn't look at her—it was his expression that bothered her. It wasn't hurt or angry, it was just blank. Again it was a struggle to keep herself from going over, hugging him and telling him everything. One glance at Tim changed her mind. He didn't seem to be looking at Patrick but from the scowl twisting his face, she knew that he was aware of the situation. She could almost feel his fists clenching every time Patrick looked over.

As soon as class ended, she put her arm around Tim's waist, both to distract him and to make Patrick angry, to keep them as far apart as she could.

"Did you do your French?" she asked him.

"Huh?" He looked down. "I don't know, part of it."

"Come on." She steered him toward the door. "You have time to copy mine."

He nodded and she allowed herself a small sigh of relief, having managed to put off whatever confrontation might be coming.

In French she sat between Tim and Beverly as usual and noticed that Beverly seemed jumpy, not looking at either one of them.

"Are you okay?" she whispered.

Beverly nodded but Susan could see that her hands were shaking.

"Well, what happened?" she asked.

"Nothing."

"Are you sure?"

Beverly nodded but Susan could see that more than her hands were trembling.

"If you want," Susan started, "I could—"

"If you wouldn't mind allowing me to teach, Miss McAllister . . ." Mr. Hanson said sarcastically.

She blushed, focusing on her notebook.

"Don't let me interrupt you," the teacher said.

She blushed again and he went back to his lecture.

After French Susan sat in her third-period study hall with Beverly, Randy and Paula, half-working on homework. Beverly still seemed nervous, fluttery almost, and the only thing that Susan knew was that her edginess had something to do with Tim. She wouldn't even have known that but after French he had gone over to Beverly, saying something very quietly, and Susan had seen her flinch. Now, in study hall, Susan kept an eye on Randy, who didn't seem to know anything more than she did but looked worried nonetheless.

Susan stared at her physics book for a while, then decided that it was time to start talking about LSD and see if she could get any reactions out of them, particularly from Beverly and Randy, whom she might be able to catch off guard.

"God, this is boring." She sat back, yawning and closing her book. "You know, I was wondering," she said conversationally. "Do you think Tim could get me some LSD?"

They all jumped, Paula looking predictably horrified, Randy checking to see whether anyone else had heard, Beverly just sitting stunned.

"Some what?" Beverly asked.

"LSD," Susan shrugged. "You know." She grinned. "It's a drug? Haven't you ever done it? It's really big in New York."

"Will you keep it down?" Randy asked. "Christ, you want the whole room to know?"

122

"Oh," Susan brushed his words aside. "None of them heard. Don't be such a frump. Anyway, I was just wondering. You think Tim could get some?"

"Probably not." Beverly's voice and expression were back to *sang-froid*.

"I thought he was Joe Big-Dealer," Susan said, realizing that she sounded like Patrick. "Isn't there anyone around this place who could get some?"

"There was some bad stuff going around a few weeks ago," Randy said calmly. "I don't think he'd want to take the chance."

"Boy, you should have seen it, Sue." Paula's eyes were big. "A girl died and everything! It was awful."

Susan saw both Randy and Beverly frown at Paula. She managed to keep her own expression calm and vaguely curious.

"Actually *died*?" she asked. "Was it stuff Tim sold her?"

"No," Beverly answered without hesitation. "She probably got it in the city. I never heard of anyone around here selling it."

"You should have seen it, Sue," Paula said eagerly. "She was a really good student and everything. It freaked everyone out. The police thought it was maybe even suicide!"

"Paula, come on." Beverly sounded tired. "Susan doesn't care about that."

"Yeah, but it was so awful." Paula turned back to Susan. "You should have seen it. No one even knew she took drugs, then all of a sudden—"

"You mean *you* didn't know," Beverly interrupted. "Practically everyone else did."

"Well, maybe you did," Paula said. "But a lot of other people didn't. She was valedictorian and everything, Sue."

Susan didn't say anything, praying that no one could hear her heart pounding. She had finally caught someone in a lie, in an absolute, direct lie, caught Beverly in a— She started talking, knowing

123

that if she didn't change the subject, her face was going to give her away.

"We had a guy flip out on heroin," she said, hoping that the perspiration that had started on her face wasn't as obvious as it felt. "A while before Christmas. Jumped out a window and all. I think his parents are suing the school."

"Something like that happened here too," Paula agreed. "This guy in my chemistry class—"

"For Christ's sakes, Paula!" Randy shook his head. "Can we forget about it already? I have to get this calculus done."

"I'm sorry," Paula said. "I thought she might be interested."

I'm *very* interested, Susan thought.

"You should have seen the guy at our school," she remarked. "His parents threw fits because they said they knew he'd never taken drugs or any of that and the police came and questioned everyone. It was really wild."

"Did you get questioned?" Paula asked.

"Yeah. Just about everyone did. I guess I did because I had a couple of classes with him." Susan yawned. "Far as I know, they're still trying to figure it out."

"Not here," Paula said. "The police said that Peter—he was the guy—must have gotten some bad stuff somewhere and that Colleen did too. Except they think maybe she wanted to kill herself. It was really weird."

Susan looked at the other two.

"Enough to make Tim want to close up shop, huh?" she asked.

"Didn't affect him any," Beverly said blandly. "He wasn't even selling that kind of stuff."

Yeah, Susan thought. Sure. Thank you, Paula. Thank you, dumb, over-eager Paula.

* * *

Standing at her locker, taking out her gym clothes, she felt someone come up behind her.

"Thought you might want to look at these," Patrick said.

"What?"

He handed her several postcards: the Eiffel Tower, the Alps, the Vatican; all postmarked and dated, sent by Colleen during the summer she went traveling with her parents. Susan swallowed, looking at the tall, distinctive handwriting, remembering the postcards she herself had received that summer.

"You lie lousy," Patrick said.

"Well, her parents—"

"Right," he nodded. "You going to tell me the truth?"

"I did."

He just looked at her.

"Okay, I lied about that part," she admitted. "But the rest of it is true."

He shook his head.

"It is. She—"

"Look," he cut her off, "I was asking Randy Carson some questions in homeroom today and he practically passed out when I mentioned drugs. I told him Baker found out that Tim was using drugs and was going to kick him off the team. I swear he jumped about thirty feet. Now are you going to tell me or what?"

Susan inhaled and exhaled once, thinking hard. She was never going to be able to keep him from finding out. Far better to tell him the truth than to have him poking around and maybe blow everything.

"Okay," she nodded. "I'll tell you. Come over to my house tonight and I'll tell you everything, okay?"

"What's wrong with now?"

"Tim's supposed to meet me here, that's what's wrong with now. Just come over tonight, okay? And don't talk to anyone."

"Is it about Colleen?" he asked hesitantly. "I mean, did you really find something out?"

"I'm not sure."

"But you think you did?"

"I'm not sure. Maybe."

He nodded, starting away, then coming back.

"Has everything with Tim been a fake?" he asked. "I mean, you don't really—"

She interrupted, seeing Tim heading in her direction.

"Patrick, will you leave me alone?" she asked. "I said no already!" She pushed away from him, hurrying to meet Tim.

"What'd he want?" Tim demanded.

"He just asked if I could go to a movie on Friday. I said no."

"Was that all he said?" Tim looked ready to go after him.

"Yeah, that was it." Distract him, she thought. Do something to distract him. She moved a suggestive hand across his chest. "I–I'm looking forward to this afternoon."

"Oh, yeah?" He responded to that, as she had known he would. "Gonna loosen up a little this time?"

"I might."

"Yeah?" He grinned, then turned serious. "What's this I hear about you wanting some LSD?"

"I asked them if they thought you could get it." She leaned closer, lowering her voice. "It's really excellent."

"Yeah, but I can't—"

"Can you get heroin?" she asked. "Mescaline? Mushrooms?"

He nodded.

"And you can't get LSD? Who're you kidding? If you're scared, why don't you admit it?"

"I'm not scared!" he said, offended.

"Yeah, sure."

126

"Okay," he nodded. "You want it so bad, I'll get it. What would you say if I already had some?"

"I wouldn't believe you." She took her knapsack out of her locker, noticing the postcards in her hand and shoving them far in, out of sight.

"What're those?" He reached up his hand to take them out.

"From a friend of mine." Susan shot her hand up to block his.

"Can I see them?"

"No." She closed the locker, walking down the hall.

"What, are they from that guy?" He came with her. "The one from New York?"

"Just from a friend of mine."

"Yeah, I bet."

"Changing the subject?" she asked.

"No. If you want it, I've got it. I've had it for a while."

"How much? I've got plenty of—"

"We'll work it out." His eyes went down over her body and he grinned, putting his arm around her waist. "We'll figure out something."

"Wait a minute." She stopped walking. "This isn't the stuff you sold to that girl, is it?"

"What?" He stopped too. "What girl?"

"That girl Colleen or whatever her name was." Susan tried not to swallow visibly. "The one who was killed."

"I didn't sell it to her!" His eyes were wide with defensive fear. "Who says I sold it to her?"

"I don't know." She started walking again, knowing that he shouldn't be reacting this way, shouldn't be reacting this much, knew it even as the trembling started through her body.

"Get back here!" He yanked her over against the lockers, gripping her arms above the elbow, his face flushed. "Who told you that?"

"I–I don't know." She tried to squirm free. "Let go, that hurts."

"Who told you?"

"I–I don't know." My God, he killed her. He must have killed her. I can't believe he killed her. "Randy and Beverly, I think."

"No, they didn't. Who said that? Was it Finnegan?" He shook her. "Damn it, Susan, tell me!"

"Maybe it was Paula, I don't know."

"Paula?" His voice was irritated and disbelieving. "It wasn't *Paula.*"

"Maybe I just figured it was you," Susan shrugged, the trembling shaking her body more than his grip had. "You're always bragging about being the big dealer around here and I just figured—"

"Well, I didn't, okay? And I don't want to hear you saying that again, got it?"

"You did though," she said softly. "That's why you're doing this, right? Because you did."

"I didn't. I just . . ." He released her. "I–I thought I did for a while. I'd sold her some other stuff but then I found out another guy sold her the LSD."

Another lie, Susan thought, leaning against a locker for support. Oh, God, they're really all involved.

"I just didn't want to get mixed up in it, that's all," he said. "I mean, Christ, you can understand that."

Susan closed her eyes, trying to control herself.

"Hey, come on," he said. "I'm sorry. You just sounded like that guy Finnegan. I didn't mean to get mad."

He killed her, Susan thought, her eyes shut. He actually killed her. She didn't know how yet, she didn't know why, but she knew that he had done it. She had to hang on, somehow she had to hang on. She couldn't let him know—

"Oh, come on." He put his arms around her. "I'm sorry. I didn't mean to take it out on you. I've been

128

worried about that guy Finnegan and—well, don't be mad."

She tried to breathe normally, to keep her heart from pounding, her expression from giving her away. She had to stay in control, she couldn't let him know—

"Hey." He rested his hands on her shoulders, the contact bringing her close to nausea. "You're already late. Let's just skip out. We'll go for a ride. You want to do that?"

She shook her head, her eyes shut tight.

"You sure?"

"I have to go to class," she said unsteadily.

"But you're already late."

"I don't care."

"Well, okay." He walked her down to the locker room, Susan concentrating all her energies on keeping under control. "I'll stop by for you after, okay?" He flashed the cocky grin. "Don't be mad, huh?"

129

CHAPTER SIXTEEN

SUSAN SANK against the locker-room door, weak and dizzy. He couldn't have killed—how could he?—not Colleen—not— She stumbled inside the locker room, pain riffling through her stomach. Lurching past a group of girls just inside, she made her way to an empty bench. She slumped over, burying her elbows in her stomach, trying to ease the pain.

The room was buzzing with conversation and changing until everyone began to stare uneasily at Susan, then at each other.

"Wh–what's wrong with her?" a girl asked, her voice nervous.

"It's probably drugs," another girl said. "I bet anything it's drugs."

"I'll go get Miss Jenkins." The first girl hurried toward the gym teacher's office.

"Wait." Beverly moved in front of her. "What if it isn't? Give the kid a break."

"What if it is? What if it's like Colleen?" the girl asked and everyone else nodded.

"Yeah, and what if it isn't? Just keep Jenkins out of here." Beverly crossed the locker room. "I'll take care of it."

"What are you going to do?" a girl asked nervously.

"Find out what's wrong with her, what else?" She crouched down, touching Susan's shoulder. "What is it?" she whispered fiercely.

Susan didn't answer, breathing hard and bent over.

"What is it?" Beverly grabbed her arm, pulling her up, and stared at the perspiration on her face. "Jesus, what happened? Are you okay?"

Susan shook her head.

"Well, come here." Beverly pulled her to the back of the locker room, past the staring class, giving them a "She's-new-and-someone-has-to-help-her" look.

"Anything wrong, girls?" The gym teacher came out of her office at the front of the locker room, hearing the sudden silence.

Beverly shot one of the girls a look.

"N–no, Miss Jenkins," the girl said.

The teacher frowned, unconvinced. She looked around, then zipped up her warm-up jacket.

"Okay, girls," she said. "Hurry up and change and get out to the gym." She strode through the swinging doors to the gymnasium.

As the doors closed, everyone looked at Beverly, who by now had taken Susan to a bench in the back of the room.

"Hey, you heard her," she said.

Uneasy, they continued changing.

"You need help?" a girl ventured.

"No," Beverly shook her head. "I think she's just high." She bent down. "Are you sick?" she whispered. "You want to go to the nurse?"

Susan shook her head, still breathing hard but beginning to calm down.

"Did you take something?"

Susan nodded.

"What was it? Do you know what it was?" Beverly shook her a little, trying to get a response, and Susan thought of Tim. "How much did you take?"

Susan kept breathing hard, realizing that Beverly had given her an opening and all she had to do was play along with it.

"How much, Susan?" Beverly's voice was edged.

"I–I don't know," she gasped.

"Susan!"

"It's getting better." Susan dragged her sleeve across her face, feeling perspiration. "They just hit hard."

"What was it?"

"I–I don't know. I was stupid, I didn't eat all day." She rested her face in her arms. "I didn't know they were that strong."

"How many did you take?"

"I don't know, two."

"Well, God, are you okay?"

"I don't know. I think so." Susan shook her head, still trembling.

"What was it?"

"I–I don't know. They were blue."

"Come on, girls!" Miss Jenkins called from the door.

Most of the class headed out.

"What do you mean, blue?" Beverly asked.

"I don't know. That's what color they were." Susan moved her hair back. "Look, I'll get dressed. You go out there. I don't want you getting in trouble because of me."

"And what do I do, tell her there's some kid in here tripping out?"

"If you want."

Beverly stared at her, then shook her head.

"Well, are you okay?" she asked, exasperated.

"I think so." Susan gestured toward the door. "Really, go."

"God." Beverly let out her breath. "You're really weird, Susan, you know that? Jesus!" She stared at her for another second and then ran out to the gym.

Alone, Susan sank forward, covering her face

with her hands. "Colleen," she whispered, "I'm scared. What do I do? I'm really scared."

After a minute she managed to stand up, leaning heavily against a locker. She stumbled back to the bench where she had left her knapsack, knowing that she had to change and get out there.

When she finally emerged, Miss Jenkins looked irritated.

"About time," she said. She gestured toward an empty spot in one of the volleyball teams. "Get in the game!"

Still shaking, Susan took the spot. It happened to be next to Beverly.

"How do you feel?" Beverly muttered.

"I'm really up." Susan put on a dazed smile. "Let me know if the ball comes near us."

"Terrific."

For a couple of minutes Susan paid attention to the game, praying that the ball wouldn't come near her, knowing that she wouldn't be able to hit it.

"Thanks for helping me in there." She changed to a weak smile. "Guess I kind of freaked out."

"Guess you did," Beverly agreed, hitting the ball up to the front line. She glanced over. "Forget it." She shook her head. "You look so damn different when you smile."

"I do?"

"Yeah," Beverly nodded. "Freaks *me* out." She turned her attention back to the game. "You really remind me of someone. Only I can't figure it out."

Susan erased her smile, praying that Beverly wasn't going to pick now, of all times, to recognize her. The hurtling ball glanced off her shoulder and she reacted late, turning to go after it as the rest of the team exchanged glances.

"You going to Tim's later?" Beverly asked when they were back in the locker room.

133

"Yeah," Susan said, tight-lipped. "Far as I know."

"Then I'll see you there." Beverly closed her locker. "I'd better hurry. Yearbook meeting tonight—we've got a deadline." She rolled her eyes. "Boring!" She started for the door but paused. "Watch yourself, will you?"

"Yeah." Numbly Susan pulled her blazer on over her sweater and shirts.

She took a long time to get ready, not standing up to leave until the girls' basketball team came in noisily to change for practice. She stood up then, fumbling for her books and gym clothes. She shoved them into her knapsack, zipping it up on her way out the door. A few girls looked at her curiously but no one said anything.

Tim was leaning against the wall, tense and angry.

"What took you so long?" he demanded.

She shrugged.

"Well, you still mad at me?"

She managed to shake her head.

"Good," he nodded, looking as though he didn't really care either way. "Look, I gotta do something. Can I meet you at my house instead?"

"I guess—"

"Good," he nodded. " 'Bout an hour?"

"I guess so." She swallowed, something about his businesslike distraction making her nervous. "But can't I come with you?"

"I have to take care of something. And no, you can't come with me."

"Yeah, but—"

"Susan," he gritted his teeth. "Just meet me at my house, okay? Can we just do that?"

She nodded slowly.

"Good." He went down the hall. "See you later."

She clutched her knapsack, watching his quick steps. He was so calm, so determined, so cold—she

134

thought of Patrick suddenly. "I was asking Randy Carson some questions in homeroom today," he had said. "He practically passed out when I mentioned drugs. I swear he jumped about thirty feet." Then she remembered Tim: "Who said that? Was it Finnegan? Damn it, Susan tell me!" She thought about all of that and realized with a flash that Patrick was in trouble, deep trouble. She had to find him right away, had to warn him—

"Hi, Susan!" Paula came up behind her, smiling.

Susan nodded, fighting the paranoia behind the thought that Tim had sent her, sent Paula to make sure that she didn't have a chance to—

"The party's going to start later, did you hear?" Paula asked.

"Where's Tim? Have you seen him?"

"Alan said he had to 'do something.' " Paula stressed the words with a roll of her eyes. "I don't know, I guess—Sue, are you okay?"

"No." She gave Paula her knapsack and her blazer to hold. "Do something with these, will you?"

"Where are you going?"

Patrick, she had to find Patrick. Or the office. She knew enough now. She could go to the office and tell—

"Sue, you look really funny," Paula frowned. "Are you sure you're okay?"

"I have to go to the office." She walked swiftly down the hall. "I'll see you at Tim's, okay?"

"Well, wait a minute. Should I—"

Susan shook her head, hurrying around the corner, breaking into a run.

She would try to find Patrick first, she decided. She would try to find him and if she couldn't, she would go to the office. He had a yearbook meeting today. She'd go to it and—or was it Beverly who had the yearbook meeting? Debating, he had debating practice. She would go there and—first she ran down the hall to his locker, scanning the people in the corridor, not seeing him and running again.

She ran down to their Current Issues classroom, sure that that was where the Debating Club met. She yanked the door open; everyone in the meeting looked startled.

"Has anyone seen Patrick Finnegan?" she asked, out of breath.

People shrugged or shook their heads and she closed the door, leaning against it for a second to decide what to do next. The office. The only thing she could do now was go to the office. She turned to run, almost crashing into her English teacher, Mrs. Brenner.

"Susan," she started, "are you—"

"Have you seen Patrick?"

"Well, no, I—"

Susan ran past her and down the hall toward the office. She skidded into it and up to the front desk, breathing hard.

"Yes?" the elderly secretary asked disapprovingly.

"Is Mr. Trent here? I have to talk to him!"

"I'm sorry, he's—"

"I have to talk to him!" Susan interrupted. "I mean, please," she added hastily.

"I'm sorry, he isn't—"

"Mabel!" A teacher rushed in, tie askew, face flushed. "Call an ambulance!"

"What happened?" the secretary asked, already dialing.

"Pat Finnegan. Looks like he had some kind of accident on the stairs." The teacher was behind the desk, pausing just outside Mr. Trent's door. "Roland in?"

Susan leaned heavily against the office counter, the floor threatening to come up at her. She was too

136

late. She had tried as hard as she could and she was too—through sheer will power, she managed to stay on her feet and conscious. Dimly she heard someone say something about "south staircase" and she pushed away from the counter. The effort to go out to the hall and head toward the accident took every bit of courage she had.

A crowd had already gathered and teachers were trying to keep everyone back and away from the huddle of people at the bottom of the stairs. Susan closed her eyes, remembering the last time she had seen a person lying prone on the ground.

"Has he moved yet?" a girl standing next to her whispered.

"Before," another girl nodded. "He tried to sit up."

"Okay," the basketball coach was saying quietly as another teacher covered Patrick with a blanket. "You're okay. Don't try to talk, okay?"

"Come on, everyone." Mr. Trent strode through the crowd of students. "Let's break it up. Back to your activities, everyone."

No one really moved and he gestured toward a couple of teachers, ordering them to get people to leave, before continuing his way through the group around Patrick.

"What do you think?" he asked the basketball coach.

"Well." The man stood up. "Looks like a busted flipper." He gestured to his own elbow. "Maybe a concussion, maybe some ribs." He shook his head. "He took one hell of a fall."

"No," Patrick said weakly. "I—"

"Just be still," one of the teachers next to him said. "We have an ambulance coming."

"But I—"

"Come on." The teacher tried to make him comfortable. "Try to be quiet."

137

He closed his eyes, letting his head sink back into the jackets someone had pillowed beneath him. Susan closed her eyes too, hanging onto a stair railing, waiting for the sound of a far-away siren.

CHAPTER SEVENTEEN

THE MAIN LOBBY of Massachusetts General Hospital
was noisy and congested, large and confusing. Susan
hesitated just inside the entrance, not sure where to
go. Most of the seats were taken and the area was
crowded with tense, frightened people, all waiting,
praying, making low, nervous conversation. Nurses
bustled back and forth, shouting directions at one
another. A typewriter clattered away at the front
desk, phones rang somewhere in the distance. And
above the din the intercom crackled like a strange,
disembodied god, calling a Dr. Shumaker to Ward C,
Geriatrics.

She took a deep breath and crossed through several of the groups of people waiting, looking for the
Emergency Room. She saw Mr. Trent and two of the
teachers at the far end of the room and stopped, not
wanting them to see her. Then she noticed the entrance to the Emergency Room in a hall to the left
and hurried over to the swinging doors. Two guards
stood there, beside the large red "No Admittance"
sign on the Emergency Room doors.

She was trying to figure out a way to get past the
guards when there was a commotion of attendants,
paramedics and orderlies rushing through the ambulance entrance. It was the apparent aftermath of a
serious accident and a nurse hurriedly directed them
to the Trauma Unit. Susan slipped into the cluster of
people, moving into the Emergency Room. No one
noticed her in the excitement.

139

"—right back," she heard a nurse saying in the room next to her and when the woman came out, she caught sight of Patrick lying on a high, white-sheeted bed, his eyes closed, breathing with difficulty.

As soon as the nurse was gone and she was sure that no one was watching her, she slipped into the Treatment Room, crossing to the examining table.

She swallowed, seeing the huge splint on his left arm, wondering if he were unconscious or just asleep. If only she had reached the office in time and if only Paula hadn't delayed her and—she would have been able to prevent this, been able to—

"I'm sorry," she whispered, touching his right hand.

His eyes flickered open and he stared groggily, not seeming to recognize her. Then he looked relieved, giving her a flimsy smile.

"Hi," he said.

"How do you feel?"

He groaned, closing his eyes.

"I'm sorry." She lifted his hand to her lips, then held it against her cheek, hating the painful sound of his breathing, hating the dark bruise that started at his right cheekbone and went all the way up past his temple and into his hair.

"Someone pushed me," he said weakly. "I was tying my shoe and someone—" He shook his head, then winced, his right hand dropping to his side. After a few seconds he opened his eyes. "Don't worry, I'm okay. They gave me something." He closed his eyes again, the effort of talking painful.

"I'm sorry," she whispered again, taking his hand in both of hers.

"Hey." He pulled with his hand to get her attention.

"What?"

"Are you still mad at me?"

"What?"

"You've been so mad at me." He opened his eyes, bright now with more than physical pain. "No matter what I did, you kept—" He stopped, withdrawing his hand from hers to hold his side. He looked up, his expression tired and confused. "Did I tell you I think someone pushed me?"

She nodded.

"Was it Connors?" he asked.

"I think so."

"I don't get it." He frowned, then winced, the effort of moving his eyebrows apparently hurting his head. "Because of you?"

"No." She kissed his cheek below the bruise. "Don't worry about it. We'll talk about it after they—"

"He really pushed hard." Patrick stared down at his side and arm, his expression one of bewildered exhaustion. "I mean, he really wanted to hurt me." He focused on her again. "Because of drugs?"

"Kind of. Look, don't worry about it now, we'll—"

"You're still mad at me," he said accusingly.

"Pat, I was never mad at you." She let out her breath, leaning against the bed's railing, not sure where to start to explain.

"Did you, uh," he brought his right hand clumsily up to touch her shoulder, "really find out something about her?"

She nodded, moving closer so that he would keep his hand there.

"You going to tell me?"

"He killed her," she said quietly.

"What?"

"Tim killed her. I just—" She gulped. "I just can't prove it."

"Yeah, but he—" Patrick shook his head, stunned. "I mean, how could he—"

"All I know is that he did." She pushed her hair back over her shoulders, still not sure where to start.

"See, she was right about that guy Peter and I guess Tim found out and—"

"Wait a minute." Patrick tried to sit up, winced and lowered himself. "Is he a dealer or something."

"Yeah."

"And Peter probably found out and then Colleen—" He closed his eyes. "Oh, God. And I started asking questions too."

"Yeah."

"And you could get away with it because no one knows who you are or that you knew her."

She nodded.

"I'm so damn stupid." He squinted at her dizzily. "So what do we do?"

"Find you a doctor." She glanced around. "Aren't they supposed to be in here?"

"They're waiting for X-rays. They said they'd be back in a minute." He passed his hand over his eyes, looking pale. "I'm kind of dizzy."

"I'll go get—" Susan started for the door.

"Wait." He tried to pull her back. "Tell me what you're going to do. Call the police?"

"After I get proof," she nodded.

"How're you going to get proof?"

"I'm not sure. Tim's having this party and maybe I can—I don't know."

"But," his eyebrows came together, "you'll call the police?"

"After I have something to tell them."

"Yeah, but—"

"Don't worry, I know what I'm doing," she said. I think. "Look, I'll go find a doctor."

"But wait." He was obviously still worried about the police. "You're sure you're going to—"

"Well, Mr. Finnegan." A doctor strode into the room with a sheaf of reports in his hand. "It looks as though you've—" He stopped, frowning at Susan. "What are you doing? You're not supposed to be in here."

142

"I'm sorry," Susan blushed. "I just—"

"Well, I'm afraid you'll have to wait outside."

"But Patrick needs—" She sighed, seeing the doctor's adamant expression. "Okay, I'm going." She leaned over the bed. "I'll be back later, okay? Here or at your house, okay?" She glanced at the doctor and leaned closer. "I love you," she whispered, then turned and hurried out of the room to the main emergency reception area.

She stood there for a few seconds, trembling with emotion, and jumped as someone touched her shoulder.

"I'm sorry," a nurse said. "This is a restricted area. You'll have to—"

"I'm going," she nodded, walking toward the door to the main lobby, terror building up within her as she thought about what she had to do now. She had to prove it, and yet she had no way to prove it. Somehow she had to—

"Miss McAllister?" someone called. "Wait!"

She saw Mr. Trent, who had been at the Emergency Room desk, cross toward her, tall and very stern. She gulped, her hands automatically tightening together.

"I'd like to ask you some questions," he said.

"Why?" she asked, fear increasing.

"Well, it's my understanding that you—"

She made a dash for the door, not knowing why he wanted to ask her questions and not waiting to find out.

"Hey!" Mr. Trent shouted. "Miss McAllister!"

She burst out into the hall, the two guards by the door reacting quickly and coming after her. Running into the lobby, she stumbled into two nurses and glanced over her shoulder, catching sight of the guards and Mr. Trent and realizing that they would cut her off before she could reach the main entrance and the street.

She hesitated, thinking fast, and veered to the left,

143

into the hospital. Maybe this wasn't such a great idea, she thought as she rushed down the crowded corridor, dodging around people. Don't panic! Try not to panic.

Seeing a bank of elevators, she skidded to a stop. None of the doors was open and there didn't seem to be a staircase so she ran back out to the main hall, past a flower shop, past the Admissions Office and into another wing of the hospital. She tore past the chapel and the coffeeshop, sprinting into yet another wing—a quieter, more sedate building.

She saw a door marked "Stairs" and yanked it open, pounding up three flights, wondering whether she were still being followed. She ran out onto a third-floor ward, pausing in mid-flight as she saw a nurses' station just up the silent hallway. Trying to look as though she knew where she was going and what she was doing, she strode forward.

"Miss?"

Don't panic. He's not talking to you. Be calm, be sure of yourself, keep on walking.

"Miss?" The voice was louder, more insistent.

Turn around, act pleasantly surprised, smile inquiringly. "Yes?" She saw a security guard and it took every ounce of control she had to keep from running. "Y–yes?"

"Your shoe," he pointed. "It's untied."

"Oh." Relief washed over her. "Thank you." She bent to fix the offending leather, trying not to think of Patrick at the top of the stairs, unaware that Tim was right behind him and about to—suddenly a quiet suspicion flooded her brain as she realized that the guard was still standing there, his hand resting on his nightstick. "Uh, do you know what time it is?"

He raised his left wrist, moving back his sleeve with a quick extension of his arm, checking his Timex.

"Going on to four o'clock, Miss." He frowned. "Is there anything wrong? Maybe you'd better—"

"I'm really late." She backed into the conveniently opening elevator behind her, joining two nurses who were pushing an IV tray.

Her breath seemed to be the only sound in the elevator, along with her heartbeat, as it made its smooth ascent. The nurses stared at her but said nothing, getting off on the sixth floor.

She knew that she wasn't safe on the elevator—anyone could get on, even a guard—and she would be trapped. She punched an arbitrary number, jumping out on the ninth floor only to see bright red "Surgical Floor—Authorized Personnel Only" signs all over the place. The elevator was already gone and several figures in dark turquoise gowns approached her. In their masks, pushing the sheet-covered instrument trays, they looked particularly ominous and she backed away, jabbing the "Down" button as hard as she could.

"You aren't supposed to—" Which one of them was speaking?

"I got off on the wrong floor." She hit the button hard, with no response.

They were almost upon her. They could pull out the scalpels, they could—she pushed away from the elevator and ran down the hall, searching for an exit. She found one, jerked the door open and almost tumbled down the first flight of stairs in her panic. She raced down two flights, her breath coming in short gasps, stopping in horror as she saw a squat, thickly built man coming toward her, a small, wrinkled bag gripped in one hand. He was wearing stained grey pants and a flannel shirt. Her eyes widened and she retreated a step, clutching at the railing.

"Whatsa matter, girlie?" He continued coming up and she saw black, ragged fingernails.

"Don't touch me!" She flattened against the wall. "I wasn't—"

She bolted up the stairs away from him, stumbling and slamming her shin at the top. She picked herself up and kept running, falling against a door at the end of the last flight—eleventh? twelfth?—that had a large red "Not an Exit" sign on it. She leaned against the thick metal door, resting her head on her arms, panting and flushed from exertion.

What if the man was following her? Her head snapped up, exhaustion forgotten. She held her breath, listening, every muscle rigid. Hearing nothing, she slowly started down, jumping out at the first non-surgical floor she came to and making herself walk—not run—down the cool, green hall.

She found an elevator and stepped into it just as the doors were closing. She stared at the floor, clinging to the metal bar on the side with both hands.

"Uh, what floor?" the only other occupant, a man, asked.

She shook her head.

"Are you all right?"

She made herself nod.

"Do you know what floor you're going to?"

"First," she whispered. Outside. To the subway. To Cambridge.

CHAPTER EIGHTEEN

PATRICK LET the nurses sit him up on the examining table as the doctor wound tight tape around his ribs while the huge cast covering his arm, which was broken in one place and cracked in another, dried. It hurt him to breathe and the tape made the pain worse but he didn't say anything, too dizzy and exhausted to protest. A slight concussion, the doctor had said, adding that they might want to keep him overnight for observation.

"—finally got in touch with your mother," the doctor was saying. "She's on her way over."

Patrick nodded, too tired to answer.

"—one hell of a fall, didn't you?"

"Yeah." He thought about Tim, thought about Susan, thought about everything she had told him. It didn't make sense. He had been so dizzy when she was trying to tell him what she had found out that only part of her story had reached him. He closed his eyes, all the things she had said blurring even more.

"—you okay?" one of the nurses asked.

"Yeah." It just didn't make sense. How could Tim be a dealer? For that matter, how could he be a killer? At least she had promised that she would call the police. He would be really worried if she hadn't. She had promised, hadn't she? What had she said? "After I get proof." And something about a party. She had said that Tim was having a party and that she was going to go and—but if he was having a party and he was the killer and she was going to try to— Suddenly everything she hadn't told him began to make sense and he sat up straight, an incredible fear starting.

"I'm sorry." The doctor stopped taping. "Did I hurt you?"

Patrick shook his head. "How long's this going to take?" he asked, surprised to hear that his voice was shaking.

"A few more minutes, why?" The doctor grinned. "Hot date?"

Patrick shook his head.

"By then your mother should be here," the doctor went on. "And I'll talk to her about whether or not we're going to keep you overnight."

Patrick nodded, not really listening. He had to get out of here. He had to figure out a way out so he could reach Tim's house before—he had to get to Susan.

The doctor finished taping, gave him a friendly pat on the shoulder and turned to give one of the nurses her instructions. Patrick gripped the edge of the table with his good hand, trying to think of a way to escape before his mother arrived.

"Do you have a bathroom?" he asked.

"Sure," one of the nurses smiled at him. "But are you sure that you—"

"Yeah." He looked at the doctor. "I really do."

"No problem," the doctor nodded. "Let's get you a wheelchair and—"

"I'm fine," Patrick said. "I'd really rather not have one."

"Well, let's see." The doctor helped him up and Patrick smiled at them even as the resulting wave of dizziness threatened to knock him down.

"See?" he asked. "I'm fine."

"Okay," the doctor smiled back. "It's not far anyway. But if you get dizzy, they're putting you in a chair whether you like it or not, okay? Jane, give him a hand."

"Wait." Patrick hesitated. "Can I put on my shirt first?"

"You mean what's left of it?" one of the nurses asked and he remembered that they had had to cut it off of him.

"Well, can I put on something else then?" he asked. "I'm kind of embarrassed to go out there like this."

"A good-looking kid like you?" the doctor laughed. "What's the matter, afraid your girl will see you?"

"Yeah," Patrick smiled weakly.

They went to a Men's Room just outside the Emergency Room and he glanced around, noticing a couple of guards and an otherwise fairly empty hallway and gauging the distance to the main lobby and escape. He could make it. If he could run fast enough and take the guards by surprise, he could make it.

"You know," he leaned his good hand against the wall, "could you maybe have them get me a wheelchair after all?"

"Are you okay?"

"Just a little dizzy. I think I'd rather ride back." He started to open the door. "I'll go in here while you're gone."

She turned to call for an orderly. It distracted the guards and he made his move. He ran toward the lobby, plunging through the waiting people, keeping his eyes on the blurring red of the Exit sign.

"Hey, you!" someone yelled. "Stop!"

He ran faster, lurching against the door and into the cold January afternoon, his side throbbing excruciatingly. He shoved people out of the way with his cast, ignoring his protesting legs.

He knew that there was a taxi stand around somewhere and he looked for a row of yellow, locating it and stumbling toward the cars. He yanked open the back door of the nearest one and fell inside.

"Hey, uh—" the cabbie began, almost swallowing

149

his toothpick and swiveling around to stare at Patrick lying across the seat.

"Get out of here!" Patrick lifted himself off the torn vinyl upholstery. "Make it quick!"

"But—" The cabbie watched the guards and nurses swarm out of the hospital.

"Damn it, go!"

One look at Patrick's face, taut with determination, and the man started the engine, stepping on the gas and swerving out of the parking place.

Patrick caught a glimpse of angry, yelling faces through the window as the cab tried to pull away. Hands banged on the side of the car and someone managed to open the door. They jumped out of the way as the car careened forward, the door swinging wildly. Patrick reached out a weak right arm and pulled it shut.

"Look, pal, you know what you're doing?" the cabbie yelled, his eyes glued to the rear-view mirror. "You escaping or sumpthing?"

"Yeah," Patrick nodded, his hand braced against the back of the front seat to keep himself upright.

"Look, I don't want trouble with no police. I—"

"The police," Patrick agreed. "Good idea." He fell against the back seat, breathing hard, his head, side and heart pounding. "Take me to a phone booth and I'll tell you where to go after that." He paused. "Please."

Susan found herself leaving the hospital through the Eye and Ear Infirmary, coming out by Storrow Drive. She glanced over at the Charles River, covered by waving shadows of dusk, and took a deep breath, almost as though trying to inhale the tranquility.

She headed toward the Charles Street subway entrance, dropping a token in the turnstile and climbing up into the open-air station to wait for the next train to Harvard Square.

Shivering in the winter wind blowing off the river, she suddenly remembered that her ski jacket was in her locker at school and that she had given Paula her blazer to hold along with her knapsack. She pulled up the collars of her turtleneck and Oxford shirt, huddling into her sweater, wishing that it were heavier.

The Red Line train ground to a stop and she followed the crowds of off-duty nurses and doctors onto the already packed car, grabbing onto one of the metal poles at the side of the car for support.

Maybe it wasn't such a great idea to go to Tim's house. Maybe—no, it would be fine. They had no idea who she really was so everything would be fine. Easy even. She would go to his house, they'd all be stoned, she'd get him off into another room and then—and then what? Get him to confess? Or confide? Maybe confide was a better word. He trusted her, right? It would be easy, right? Right.

She hung onto the metal pole with both hands, the ride seeming longer than usual, longer and darker. When the train finally stopped at Harvard Station, she stepped out onto the slick cement platform, letting the crowd waft her toward the steps to the street.

On the sidewalk above the station people flowed steadily through the Square, spilling over into the street. She felt detached, isolated, as though this cheerful celebration of early evening in the Square were taking place on another planet. An earnest young man handed her a sheet of paper advertising a sale on stereo components; a girl in a bandana gave her a pamphlet on "Hunger in the Third World." She took both, automatically putting them in her pocket, feeling for her change to make sure that she had enough for a bus.

Finding that she did, she hunched her shoulders against the wind and walked through the exhaust-stained snow toward Harvard Gate, where the buses stopped. Tim's house was about a mile away and since she didn't have enough money for a taxi, the bus was probably her best bet.

Deciding that the Belmont bus was the one she wanted, she joined the crowd waiting at the gate.

"Ahlington Heights! Ahlington Heights!" a man in a uniform announced in Boston accents.

Susan rubbed her numb hands and stared through the huge iron gate into Harvard Yard, thinking about her father's rumpled old sweatshirt. Absently she watched students traversing the well-shoveled paths while her thoughts focused on what she was going to do when she reached Tim's house. Getting him into a room alone would be easy, but then what? What if he wouldn't tell her anything? Suppose he denied everything, suppose—there didn't seem to be any other way to get proof unless he confessed. There couldn't have been any witnesses, so if he didn't confess, that was it; he would never be caught.

She chafed her arms to get some heat back into them, her teeth chattering against each other, the wind seeming worse than ever. There had to be a way to—

"Medford, Medford!" the Transit Authority man announced, creating a stir in the crowd, and several students in Tufts University jackets moved forward to take Bus 96.

—prove it other than if he confessed.

Relax, she told herself, shivering. Take it easy, it's all going to work out fine. He'll tell you. He likes you, he trusts you—

"Last call, Medford!"

—so, of course, he'll tell you. But what if he doesn't? If he had killed twice—if he was cold-blooded enough to do that—then he was cold-blooded enough to deny everything. She would have to have another plan set up so that if he didn't confess, he would still be caught.

She shoved her hands into her pockets in hopes of

thawing them out. There had to be another way to prove it, there had to be some other way to—she staggered back against the icy gate, the idea suddenly dawning.

"Park Circle!" the Transit Authority man shouted.

There *was* one other way to prove it, and that was if—

"Park—"

—if it happened—

"Circle!"

—again.

"I can't," she whispered. The only way it could happen again would be if— "I can't." But that would prove it to the police since she had already told Patrick. Except that she wouldn't have to do that. She would just go to his house, get him to confess and—

She walked into the street, oblivious to the traffic, unflinching as horns blared and brakes squealed.

"Young lady, get out of the street. You'll—"

"Outta the way, ya stupid—"

She started to run, dodging past cars and the subway construction in the middle of the road and reaching the other side of Massachusetts Avenue.

"Belmont!" the Transit Authority man yelled. "Belmont!"

She ran down Garden Street, past the Harvard Common, her breath coming in short, white bursts. She turned onto Concord Avenue, narrowly avoiding parked cars, and took a left on Craigie Street, running deep into the residential center. When she was finally on Tim's street, she stumbled to a stop, leaning dizzily against a telephone pole.

"I can't do this," she said aloud. "I really can't do this."

She would go in, no one else would be there yet; he would tell her everything and—suddenly she thought about Colleen, thought of the bright, penetrating eyes, the contagious laugh, the self-deprecatingly well-bred voice. "You can do it," the voice was saying, using the calm, assured tone that Colleen had mastered to perfection. "Susan, you can do it."

"I can't. I really can't." She closed her eyes, trying to muster her courage. She thought about being eleven and playing Detective with Colleen. She remembered creeping down the hallway of her old apartment. About halfway down, she stopped, motioning for Colleen to get behind her, pulling an imaginary gun from her imaginary holster as they approached the slightly ajar door to Susan's bedroom.

"Cover me!" Susan said, holding the gun up and ready.

Colleen drew hers and Susan slunk up ahead until they were next to the room, standing on opposite sides of the doorway. Susan nodded at Colleen, then lifted her leg, kicking the door open and bursting into a quiet, messy bedroom. She looked around, her gun out, decided that the room was safe and replaced the imaginary gun in its imaginary holster while motioning Colleen in with her other arm.

"All clear," she said.

"Good work." Colleen came in, replacing her gun as well. "Nice work, Linc."

"Thanks for covering me, Julie."

"Julie?" Colleen paused in the act of sitting down on the bed. "I thought I was being Pete."

"Thanks for covering me, Pete." Susan sighed. "Wouldn't it be neat to really *be* in the Mod Squad?"

"Yeah," Colleen agreed. "It must be neat to solve mysteries."

"I bet we could do it. Like," Susan paused to think, "like, I bet we could solve a murder!"

"You'd be too scared," Colleen snorted.

"You're right," Susan said quietly, pushing away from the telephone pole, her teeth knocking together in the cold as she remembered the two confident little eleven-year-olds. "I *am* too scared."

She ran down the snowy street and up Tim's driveway to the front steps, her teeth chattering more than ever. She straightened her hair with one hand, then opened the front door, hearing loud music coming from upstairs.

The party had already started.

CHAPTER NINETEEN

SHE WALKED slowly up the stairs, concentrating on what she was going to do and how she was going to do it. Stopping at the third floor, she sucked in her breath, trying to summon the courage to walk down the hall. She took a hesitant step forward, then glanced up at the ceiling.

"Cover me," she whispered. Taking a deep breath, she started down the hall, pushing the last door open and trying to ignore the buzzing in her ears.

Tim, Randy, Alan and Paula were in the dimly lit room, all looking very stoned. The stereo was blasting. Alan and Paula were on one couch, making out between tokes. Randy slouched in the beanbag chair near the stereo, focusing blearily at her as though trying to decide whether she were Beverly or not.

" 'Bout time you showed up," Tim drawled from the other couch, his eyes heavy-lidded. "C'mon over here and sit down." He patted his leg suggestively.

"Hi." She smiled nervously at the others, who didn't seem to notice, and went over to the couch, where she perched on the edge.

"What took you so long, babe?" Tim draped his arm around her waist, pulling her closer.

"I got held up."

"That's for sure." He nuzzled her shoulder. "Got that stuff you were asking for, babe."

"Oh, yeah?"

"Yeah. Wait a sec." He stood up with difficulty, leaning on her for support before pushing away and half-walking, half-staggering to the door. He stumbled back. "You sure you don't like dust? We got some beautiful dust."

"Beautiful," Randy agreed, laughing. "Like, just beautiful."

Tim laughed too, reaching languidly onto one of the stereo speakers, and picked up a joint after two attempts.

"Here," he grinned, handing it to her. "A Connors' Special. Wait." He fumbled for his light. "Wait, lemme—"

"Don't worry," she said. "I can do it."

"Yeah?" He tried to get the lighter going, dropping it in the process and bending down to try to find it.

"Tim, come on." She tugged at his arm. "Just sit down."

"Huh?" He squinted up at her.

"Sit down."

"Oh." He grinned. "Yeah." He sat heavily on the couch, slinging his arm around her, bringing her back against the cushions with him. "Shit," he said, grinning at nothing and clumsily stroking her hair. "I'm like, really blasted."

That's for sure, she thought, drawing away from the touch of his hand, shuddering.

"Been thinking about you," he whispered. "Wishing you were here. I was getting kinda worried you weren't coming."

"I got held up."

"Yeah?" His hands began moving. "Well, I was wondering." His hands stopped. "You cold or something, babe? You're all—" He made himself shake, imitating her.

"It's cold outside," she said weakly.

"Yeah? Well, it's winter." He laughed. "Winter's cold. January's winter, huh? Too cold for the damn groundhog even." He laughed again and she closed her eyes, wishing that he weren't quite so stoned.

"Hey." His hand fumbled through her hair to find her face. "Whatsa matter? Why you so quiet?"

"Can we go somewhere and talk?" she asked.

"What, you mean alone?"

"Yeah."

"Sure," he grinned. "Let's go." He sat up with effort. "Hey, Bev." He grinned, nodding toward the door. " 'Bout time, Bev."

Susan looked over and saw Beverly standing stiff in the doorway, clutching a thin, paperbound booklet, her eyes large with something that seemed like fear or a dazed horror.

"Hey, kid." Randy hauled himself up. "How are ya?"

Beverly didn't answer but pulled him out into the hall, and Susan felt a cold, premonitory kind of terror. When Randy reappeared in the door a minute later with an expression on his face that mirrored Beverly's, her fear grew even stronger.

"Tim." Randy's voice was hoarse. "Come here."

Tim shrugged, pushing himself to his feet.

"Right back, babe," he said, patting Susan's cheek and then making his way to the door.

Susan sat up straight on the couch, her fear mounting when Tim didn't return. She glanced at Paula and Alan, lying on the other couch and not seeming to notice anything going on around them. Looking back at the door, she saw Tim, flushed and furious, hanging onto the doorjamb.

"Get out here," he said.

She gulped, glancing at Paula and Alan, who were all over each other and didn't even look up. She stood up and went to the door, not knowing what else to do. He grabbed her arm, yanking her out of the room, gripping her arm just above the elbow.

"You'd better have an explanation for yourself, babe," he said quietly, viciously.

"I—" She wasn't able to keep her voice from shaking. "I don't know what you're talking about."

158

He jerked the booklet away from Beverly, holding it out. It was a yearbook from the Longfellow School—from the year that she and Colleen and Patrick had been in the ninth grade—and her picture was in it even though she had moved away. He flipped it open to a page showing a candid picture of her with Colleen, the two grinning happily in a crepe-papered gym and wearing costumes for the Fifties' dance.

"So?" she asked with the strong feeling that she might burst into tears.

"It's Colleen Spencer," he said.

"Yeah," she shrugged. "So? We went to school together."

"Thought you were from New York," he said.

"I am. I lived here when I was younger, that's all." She forced a trembling smile. "What's the big deal?"

"Gee, do you think Tim could get me some LSD?" Beverly's voice was bitterly mimicking and Susan swallowed, the threatening tears blurring her vision.

"You tell me, Susan," Tim moved her against the wall, "what's the deal."

"I was curious," she said. "Colleen wasn't into drugs when I knew her."

"What's that got to do with me?" he asked.

"Nothing."

"Yeah," he agreed, the hand gripping her arm sliding up to her neck, his fingers tightening around her throat. "Want to see the picture of you with Finnegan?"

She swallowed, his hand unyielding.

"Yeah," he said. "That's what I figured." He looked at Randy. "Get Alan and Paula out of here. I don't care how you do it, just get them out of here."

"Yeah, but—" Randy started.

"Do it!"

Randy nodded, going back into the other room.

"Okay," Tim said. "Let's go."

159

Blairsville High School Library

"Where?" Susan asked, trying to swallow against his hand.

He didn't answer, giving her a rough shove down the hall.

"You too," he said to Beverly. "You're part of this now."

She nodded dully, following after them. He opened the door to his bedroom, pushing Susan inside and onto a chair. Leaning over her, he grasped her face between his hands.

"Make a move, babe," he said, "and I'll break your jaw. Got it?"

She nodded and he released her, walking to his desk but not turning his back. He pulled a small container from the top drawer, dipped his index finger into it and took two quick snorts, then let out a deep breath and replaced the container.

"What are you doing?" Beverly asked from the doorway.

"Making sure I don't have to do this one straight." Slowly and deeply he inhaled twice, then shook his head and moved across the room. "Close the goddamned door, will you?" He shook his head again and laughed, sitting down on the bed. "Jesus, Susan, you had me fooled, I gotta give you that. I thought you were—" His face hardened. "Never mind what I thought. Let's hear it."

"Hear what?" she asked.

"Everything."

"There's nothing to hear." She watched his right hand turn into a fist. "Well, there isn't. I used to live here and I knew them."

"You moved right after I came," Beverly said and Susan nodded.

"So what are you doing here now?" Tim asked.

"We moved back."

"And?"

"And what?"

"What about Spencer?"

160

She didn't say anything, pressing her teeth against her lower lip, feeling it tremble.

"I want an answer!" He was on his feet now.

She shook her head and he backhanded her hard across the face. She managed not to cry out, almost managed not to flinch, and looked over at Beverly, standing by the closet and crying silent tears. She looked again at Tim, his arm raised, his fist clenched.

"*Now*, Susan," he said.

"She was my best friend," she whispered. "You killed my best friend."

"Yeah," he nodded, lowering his arm. "That's what I wanted to hear."

The door opened. "They're gone," Randy said.

Susan let her face sink into her hands, her cheek throbbing, tears close. She slouched lower, almost more exhausted than frightened.

"The police are coming," she said.

"Oh, yeah?" Tim asked and she could sense his grin.

She lifted her head. "You don't think I'd be stupid enough to come here without telling anyone, do you?" she asked.

"Yeah." He laughed, the influence of the cocaine—or whatever it was he had snorted—obvious. "You're as stupid as she was. How could you both be so god-damned stupid?" He laughed harder, going over to his desk again. He took the little container from the top drawer, uncapped it, lifted out some powder on his fingernail and took another snort with his left nostril. He closed the container, put it back and took a black tackle-box from another drawer and unlocked it.

"Oh, Christ," Randy said.

"You talking to me?" Tim flashed his grin. Then he laughed, bringing the box over to the bed. Susan sat up straighter, gripping the sides of the chair, her eyes on the door. "Not going anywhere, are you, babe?"

Susan just looked at the door, trying to figure out whose side Randy was on.

"You know," Tim became conversational, making up for the others' silence, "anything I use'll probably work if I give you too much. Hell, I could just shoot air into you—that'd probably do it."

"You don't think drugs'll look kind of suspicious?" Randy asked, standing tense against the door.

"Not if they find her in the city somewhere." Tim rummaged through the box, looking up with a grin. "Hell, they'll be happy if they can identify her, forget anything else." He turned, hearing a small gasp. "Whatsa matter, Bev? Can't take it? You didn't have to tell me about the yearbook, you know. You're part of it now."

"I didn't want Randy to get in trouble," she said shakily.

"Yeah," Tim laughed. "Who you kidding? You don't want *me* to get in trouble." His laugh was delightedly malicious. "Never got over it, did you? Still want me, don't you?" He stood up, an athletic ripple of muscles obvious through his shirt. "Right, Bev? Am I right, Bev?"

She didn't answer but stood leaning against the dresser with her back turned to them. Susan made a slow move to her feet, gauging the distance to the door, gauging Randy's attention level, supporting herself on the seat of the chair with trembling arms. Tim spun around, knocking her to the floor with a vicious shove.

"Thought I told you not to—" He stopped, seeing Beverly stride to the door, the frightened indecision gone from her posture. "Hey! Where you going?"

"To call the police," she said softly.

"You do, and I'll—"

She paused, giving him a long, bitter look. "Try

162

and stop me," she said and bolted past Randy to the hall and the stairs.

"Get her!" Tim ordered. "Damn it, move!"

"I'm going with her," Randy said and also ran, his steps loud as he pounded down the stairs.

Tim hesitated for a few seconds and Susan made a desperate lunge for the door, trying to get past him. He reacted, bringing her down in a hard tackle, his full weight on her, one hand fumbling for the black box.

"Bitch!" he panted, shoving her sweater sleeve up, ripping the Oxford shirt sleeve up after it. "Just like the other one." His face hardened. "*Both* the other ones."

Susan struggled to free herself, frightened far beyond terror, weakened by his weight and the hand he had at her throat, struggling to pull it away with both of hers.

"Just like the other one," he said again, his eyes dark and deranged, both hands at her throat now.

She fought through the beginning dizziness, the hollow rushing in her ears, wrenching at his hands, almost getting away for a second, trying to breathe, trying desperately to breathe, trying to—

"She didn't cry either," he whispered.

CHAPTER TWENTY

PATRICK STUMBLED out of the taxi and leaned against one of the trees in Tim's front yard as the driver sped away. He squinted at the dark, quiet road, failing to see any police cars. He would have to go in alone. He couldn't wait, she might be— Summoning the feeble remnants of his strength, he made his way up the front steps, falling against the door. He lurched inside, dimly hearing music—music or the ringing in his ears.

He saw Randy rushing down the stairs and he grabbed him with his good arm.

"Where is she?" he demanded hoarsely.

Randy, appearing more numb than surprised, pointed upstairs and Patrick shoved past him, sudden adrenaline coming from nowhere, taking the steps three at a time. Following the sound of music to the third floor, he heard the hard breathing and weak thuds of a struggle and he raced faster, the scuffling noises leading him to Tim's bedroom. He saw Susan on the floor, Tim with his hands at her throat, and he leaped across the room, swinging wildly with his cast.

Tim was knocked back against the wall, taken completely by surprise by the attack. He recovered fast, scrambling to his feet with the easy grace of a wrestler, his muscles bulging confidently.

"If it isn't Florence Nightingale," he sneered, lunging forward at Patrick, the force of his charge sending them both to the floor. Bigger, and not hampered by a cast, Tim easily gained the advantage, both fists swinging.

Susan managed to scramble to her knees, trying to grab him, but Tim shook her off impatiently, concentrating on Patrick, his blows thudding into the taped rib cage. He was drawing his right fist back as the sound of police sirens whined to a stop in front of the house.

All three of them froze, exchanging quick, startled stares. Then Tim jumped up, slamming the tackle box shut and shoving it under the bed, slamming desk drawers, slamming out of the room and down the hall to get rid of any other drugs that might be lying around in the open.

Patrick dragged himself to a sitting position, looking at Susan. She came over, put her arms around him, and they clung to each other, breathing hard, hearts thudding.

"Are you okay?" she asked against his ear.

"Yeah." He nodded between ragged breaths. "You?"

"Yeah." She clutched at him, her arms weak. "Thank you."

"You're kidding, right?"

She shook her head, moving closer.

"I, uh . . ." she gulped, knowing that the tears were finally coming, wanting to hold them off for a little longer. "I can't do this," she gestured toward the hall with her head. "Will you?"

He nodded and she kissed his cheek before standing up, pushing her hair back with weary hands.

"Where you going to be?" he asked.

"Where do you think?" she asked.

By hiding in a room on the second floor while the police pounded up to the third, she managed to leave the house without being seen, escaping through a sun-porch door and cutting through back yards before moving out to the street.

Cambridge was quiet and deserted, dusky and chill. She started the long, cold walk to Mount Auburn Cemetery, the wind riffling through her clothes, her Top-Siders slipping on the ice.

The iron entrance gates finally loomed up out of the darkness and she walked onto the freshly shoveled main path. Deciding not to take the time to follow it, she crunched across the snow, her shoes' icy crust dragging at her.

She saw the raised, newly dug mound long before she reached it. Misshapen and grotesque, it broke the pattern of neatly arranged tombstones in the carefully cultivated Spencer plot, a basket of flowers next to it trying bravely to survive. She kept walking and then bent down over the grave, gently brushing the dusting of fresh snow off the marker. She traced her fingers across the name, across the date of birth and across the date of—she closed her eyes.

It was over. It was finally over. And it didn't seem to make much difference because their friendship was over too, a friendship that she had treasured more than almost anything else in the world was over. She sat down on a nearby tombstone, remembering another incident from the past, this one hurting more than any of the others.

They were fourteen. Susan was about to move to New York and they were sitting on Colleen's front steps, looking at the red and gold autumn leaves covering Louisburg Square, eating chocolate-chip cookies out of the bag.

"Don't worry," Colleen said with her mouth full. "You'll remember me. I'm the fat one."

"You're not fat," Susan laughed.

"Oh, yeah?" Colleen peered into the bag of cookies. "Give me another twenty minutes."

Susan laughed again, then lost her smile, remembering what they had just been talking about. "I don't want to go," she said. "I can't believe Mom and Dad are so into it."

"It's a good job," Colleen shrugged.

"Yeah." Susan took another cookie out of the bag. "Good for everyone else." She frowned at the cookie and then threw it across the street, bouncing it off the Spencers' Mercedes.

Colleen grinned, taking out a cookie and throwing it at another car, hitting the windshield. Then both of them were throwing cookies at cars, at trees in the square, at the houses across the square—throwing cookies until the cobblestones were littered and the bag was empty.

"Don't worry," Colleen said, peering into the bag at the crumbs. "You'll remember me. I'm the emaciated one." She looked up with that wide grin. "Want to go in and get the Mallomars?"

Susan laughed, touching her friend's arm in the brief, awkward physicality of close friendship. "I'm going to miss you," she said. "I'm really going to miss you."

"Me too," Colleen said and neither spoke for a minute, each staring at the scattered cookies. "Hey," she said, returning the shy arm caress for a second, "this isn't parole, you know."

"Parole?" Susan lifted her eyebrows, confused. "What are you talking about?"

"Life sentence," Colleen answered solemnly. "I think we're stuck with each other."

"Oh, yeah?" Susan started to grin.

"Absolutely," Colleen nodded, still solemn. "For the duration." Then she looked even more solemn. "Forever."

"That sounds like a pretty long time," Susan said.

"*Very* long," Colleen agreed.

They looked at each other, trying to keep serious expressions and failing, laughing until they were almost out of breath and falling off the steps.

"We'll be—friends for life," Colleen said, laughing

167

weakly. "Even when we're old and married. Friends for—"

Friends for life, friends for life, friends for life.

Sitting on the tombstone now, hunched against the cold and the memory, Susan finally started to cry. She brought her hands up to cover her face and cried harder, remembering Colleen's voice, her face, everything about her.

Suddenly an arm and a cast wrapped around her, pulling her close.

"I'm sorry," Patrick whispered. "I'm really sorry."

She cried uncontrollably now, burying her face in his shoulder. Patrick just held her, sitting there on the tombstone and rocking her gently.

"I didn't," she tried to stop the tears, "I didn't mean to do any of that stuff to you. I didn't—"

"Don't even think about it." He kissed the top of her head, hugging her, letting her cry. "Can I tell you something?"

She nodded, resting her head on his shoulder.

"I love you," he said. "And I'm proud of you. Really, really proud of you."

She started to cry again, pressing closer and noticing his shivering as she did. She sat up, for the first time seeing that he was wearing only a hospital gown over his jeans. Still crying, she pulled her sweater over her head and wrapped it around his shoulders, tying it gently in front.

"Don't do that," he said. "It's too cold."

"That's why I did it."

"I'm fine." He put his good arm around her shoulders to keep her warm. "The police gave me a ride over here."

"Yeah?" She squinted, looking for the car in the darkness.

"Yeah." He rested his head against hers. "How about we get out of here?"

She nodded and bent to run her hand across the

marker, brushing off the few remaining flakes of snow.

"I must look terrific," she gulped.

"I never saw anyone who looked better."

She squeezed his hand, staring at the grave for a long minute. When she stood up, straightening her shoulders with an effort, he lowered his head, their lips meeting tenderly. Then they pulled apart, looked at each other, and he kissed her cheek once more before they started across the snow, each supporting the other.

EPILOGUE

LOUISBURG SQUARE was snowy, snowy and full of memories as Susan sat on the Spencers' front steps, remembering countless days and nights, mornings and afternoons, parts of her life.

She reached down, picking up a handful of snow, packing it into her gloves to form a hard ball. Colleen had always loved to throw things, especially snowballs. And no matter where she aimed, she would miss and hit something else. Aiming at Susan, she would break windows, knock off policemen's caps, dent signs. And Susan had always known that Colleen did it on purpose, that she was perfectly capable of hitting a target. Missing was just more fun.

She looked at the square, shaping the ball in her hands, remembering a summer afternoon when they were ten. As always, they had climbed over the fence to the private garden—even though Colleen's parents had a key—and were lying underneath the trees on the grass, staring up at a cloudless summer sky.

"You ever thought about what real life's going to be like?" Colleen had asked, her hands interlocked behind her head.

"Real life?" Susan had raised herself up on one elbow. "What are we doing now?"

"Trespassing," Colleen grinned. "But I mean it. Won't it be neat when we're grown up and the real stuff starts happening?"

"The real stuff?" Susan's eyebrows went up. "Have you been reading that book again?"

170

"No! That is, uh, not recently." Colleen coughed, changing the subject. "I mean when we're old and getting ready to go to college—real life, you know?"

Susan sighed, standing up and looking at the house, then out at the square. When they were old and getting ready to go to college. Like now.

She walked down to the sidewalk, noticing that the snow was starting to turn to slush. Maybe spring was thinking of coming after all. Maybe. She took a few steps down the street, tossing the snowball from one hand to the other. Suddenly, she stopped, looking up at the sky.

"Hey, Colleen!" She threw the ball up as hard as she could. "Catch!"

She waited for long seconds and the ball came plummeting down.

"I miss you," she said quietly. "I really miss you."

She took a deep breath, thinking about real life, about getting ready to go to college, and then she straightened her shoulders, walking toward Chestnut Street.

ELLEN EMERSON WHITE grew up in Narragansett, Rhode Island. She is currently a senior at Tufts University, where she is pursuing a double major in English and education. FRIENDS FOR LIFE is her first novel.

FLARE NOVELS BY
Ellen Emerson White

FRIENDS FOR LIFE 82578-3/$2.95 U.S./$3.50 Can.
A heart-wrenching mystery about Susan McAllister, a high school senior whose best friend dies—supposedly of a drug overdose. Her efforts to clear her friend's reputation and identify the killer bring her closer to the truth—and danger.

THE PRESIDENT'S DAUGHTER
88740-1/$2.95 U.S./$3.50 Can.
When Meg's mother runs for President—and wins—Meg's life becomes anything but ordinary as she works to preserve the constantly changing relationship she has with her mother—a woman who happens to be President.

ROMANCE IS A WONDERFUL THING 83907-5/$2.50 U.S./$3.50 Can.
Trish Masters, honor student and all-around preppy, falls in love with Colin McNamara—the class clown. As their relationship grows, Trish realizes that if she can give Colin the confidence to show his true self to the world, their romance *can* be a wonderful thing.

WHITE HOUSE AUTUMN
89780-6/$2.95 U.S./$3.95 Can.
In the sequel to THE PRESIDENT'S DAUGHTER, Meg struggles to lead a normal life as the daughter of the first woman President of the United States, until a shocking event makes life at the White House even more difficult.

AVON Paperbacks

Buy these books at your local bookstore or use this coupon for ordering:
....
Avon Books, Dept BP, Box 767, Rte 2, Dresden, TN 38225
Please send me the book(s) I have checked above. I am enclosing $_____
(please add $1.00 to cover postage and handling for each book ordered to a maximum of three dollars). Send check or money order—no cash or C.O.D.'s please. Prices and numbers are subject to change without notice. Please allow six to eight weeks for delivery.

Name _____

Address _____

City _____ State/Zip _____

EEW 1/90

NOVELS FROM AVON 🔥 FLARE

CLASS PICTURES	61408-1/$2.95 US/$3.50 Can

Marilyn Sachs
Pat, always the popular one, and shy, plump Lolly have been best friends since kindergarten, through thick and thin, supporting each other during crises. But everything changes when Lolly turns into a thin, pretty blonde and Pat finds herself playing second fiddle for the first time.

BABY SISTER	70358-1/$2.95 US/$3.50 Can

Marilyn Sachs
Her sister was everything Penny could never be, until Penny found something else.

THE GROUNDING OF GROUP 6	83386-7/$3.25 US/$3.75 Can

Julian Thompson
What do parents do when they realize that their sixteen-year old son or daughter is a loser and an embarrassment to the family? Five misfits find they've been set up to disappear at exclusive Coldbrook School, but aren't about to allow themselves to be permanentaly "grounded."

TAKING TERRI MUELLER	79004-1/$2.75 US/$3.50 Can

Norma Fox Mazer
Was it possible to be kidnapped by your own father? Terri's father has always told her that her mother died in a car crash—but now Terri has reason to suspect differently, and she struggles to find the truth on her own.

RECKLESS	83717-X/$2.95 US/$3.50 Can

Jeanette Mines
It was Jeannie Tanger's first day of high school when she met Sam Benson. Right from the beginning—when he nicknamed her JT—they were meant for each other. But right away there was trouble; family trouble; school trouble—could JT save Sam from himself?

Buy these books at your local bookstore or use this coupon for ordering:
....

Avon Books, Dept BP, Box 767, Rte 2, Dresden, TN 38225
Please send me the book(s) I have checked above. I am enclosing $_____
(please add $1.00 to cover postage and handling for each book ordered to a maximum of three dollars). *Send check or money order*—no cash or C.O.D.'s please. Prices and numbers are subject to change without notice. Please allow six to eight weeks for delivery.

Name _____

Address _____

City _____ State/Zip _____